FRACTURED NATION

Sunrise of Chaos—Book One

AIDAN MCCOLLUM

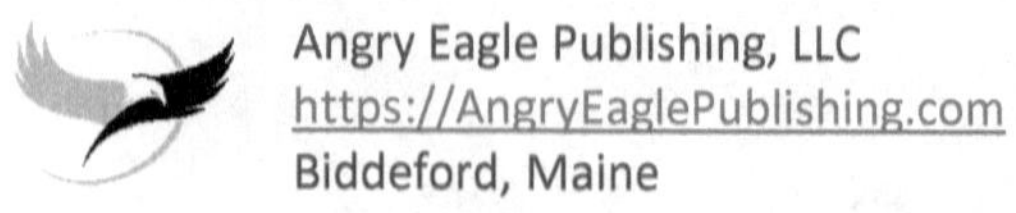

Angry Eagle Publishing, LLC
https://AngryEaglePublishing.com
Biddeford, Maine

First published by Angry Eagle Publishing 2025
Cover design by DauntlessCoverDesign.com

Paperback ISBN: 978-1-964884-21-9

This book is a work of fiction. The characters are imaginary, and any resemblance to actual persons is accidental. However, some places are based upon actual locations, but all incidents and events are fictional.

<u>Don't forget to sign up for the spam free newsletter</u>

https://bit.ly/3KmAGjh

Contents

Chapter 1
Parker Davidson

It was the final class of the day and Parker was ready to get it over with. The only thing he could think about was that this was his last summer break before senior year and a job. He'd already been doing a job online. He was making quite a bit of money, but not nearly enough to live independently.

He let out a sigh and rolled his eyes at the monotone voice of the teacher. *Doesn't she know it's the last day? No one listens to anything on the last day. This class is so boring. Why did I pick it? No way I'll be doing this next year.*

His mind danced from subject to subject and even wondered if his eyes rolled any more would it be possible to look at his brain from inside of his skull.

He heard a slight cough and found his focus wandering instead toward his girlfriend, Sydney. She smiled at him before looking back toward the front of the class. She loved art. Parker didn't, but followed her lead and did the same, trying to tune back into whatever the teacher was talking about.

His whole body leaned to the side as he rested his head in the palm of his hand, still wondering why art history was important. He'd only taken it because he thought it would be an easy A and, of course, because Sydney was in the class. He was seriously rethinking his life choices right now.

That final was hard, and he probably would have failed if Sydney hadn't helped him study. In an attempt to appear at least somewhat interested, he scribbled a quick note even though it didn't mean anything.

The teacher finally finished the lesson. "Alright, class, pack your things but wait for the bell before bolting for the door and leaving this place in the rearview. Have a great summer, and I hope to see you all next year."

She seemed to look right at Parker, who thought; *Yeah, right. There ain't no way anyone is dragging me into this class in my last year. I'll be looking for a study hall or something to take up that time.*

Parker quickly shut his notebook and stuffed it into his bag. He looked at the clock and saw that it was almost noon. Half days were even better when there was no school the next. He started counting down the seconds as the skinny hand clicked through the numbers. One by one they ticked off the seconds in slow motion.

Three, two, one. RING!!!!!!

He launched himself from his seat, snatched Sydney by the hand and beelined it for the door, dragging Sydney along behind him in a rush to escape the exodus. The hall, crowded with students and teachers, was louder than a football game in the final seconds.

Overall, this year was good but boring. Thank God next year is the last.

He burst through the door at home, flinging his backpack into the closet where he expected it would remain until next year and made his way into the living room to relax. In a side leap with all the grace of Dumbo before he realized he could fly; he flung himself over the back of the sofa and grabbed the remote to check out what was happening in the world.

His stomach growled, and he remembered there was no lunch on half days. "Oh, yeah. It's pizza rolls, chips and that last Dr. Pepper for me. I'm celebrating."

As he was about to get up, his phone chimed with a message. *Hey, you wanna grab some food to celebrate the end of our junior year?*

Parker quickly responded. *Sure, where do you want to go?*

How about Cracker Barrel? Her reply came quickly, like she'd already typed it, and he knew she really wanted to go there.

He quickly typed back, *Sure, that works. I haven't been in a while.* It wasn't one of Parker's favorites though Sydney would eat it daily if she could. Taking art classes, going to Cracker Barrel... He'd do that and more if she wanted him to. She meant the world to him, and he wanted to make her happy.

He completely abandoned all thoughts of pizza rolls or chips and hurried to change. By the time he arrived at Sydney's house, she was standing on the porch waiting for him, her school backpack in hand.

"What's in the bag? School's over," Parker teased.

"Some clothes, don't have a reason to be here if my mom is gone."

Before they even entered the restaurant, it was clear they weren't the only ones with the same idea. The parking lot was full, and he had to park way out back where the campers and trucks were. They pushed through the crowd to give their names to the hostess, who quickly seated them, much to their surprise. It helped to be one of the few parties of two.

A perky waitress walked over immediately asking, "Hi, my name is Chelsey, and I'll be your server today. Can I get you guys started off with some drinks?"

"I'll just have a Coke," Parker said.

"And for you, hun?" she asked, shifting her attention to Sydney.

"Um, I'll have a Coke, too."

Chelsey nodded and took their food orders before disappearing into the back.

"So, what are we doing today?" Sydney asked with a growing smile on her face.

"Not sure. I was thinking of going to Walmart to get a few things and maybe get some work done," Parker replied. "You would be surprised how much I'm making with this random internet stuff."

"What do you even do?"

"I do things for companies that are simple and easy to do. I learned it all online and now it's making me a ton of money, so I'm not complaining."

"Boring," she joked. "Well, I'll go with you to

Walmart and then back to your house."

Chelsey set their plates down, and they both dug in, enjoying every bite. It wasn't pizza rolls, but it tasted good. He hadn't realized how hungry he was.

While they were eating, their friend Leo walked up with his girlfriend.

"Hey, guys. Pull up a chair. Hungry?" Parker said, waving them over.

"You guys glad this year is over?" Leo asked.

They both nodded between bites and laughed.

"So, what are you planning to do this summer?" Leo asked as they sat down.

"I don't know just yet. I think I'll just hang out and work. What are you planning on doing?"

"Probably just hanging around. I don't have much else to do. I figured we needed to celebrate being done with another year of school somehow," Leo replied.

"Great minds, am I right?" Parker said, waving his hand animatedly in a wide arc indicating the full house.

It wasn't too long before Parker and Sydney were done and excused themselves.

"Well, I'm sure we'll get together sometime this week. Have a good one."

"Bye," Sydney said, waving.

"Will do, have a good one," Leo replied just as their food arrived.

"That was great. We haven't been there in a while," Sydney said, as they made their way through the double doors into the parking lot.

"I didn't even realize I was hungry till the food got there."

They returned to the truck and took the back roads over to the store before hopping on the highway to head back to the house. Parker and Sydney were both alone at home since both of their moms, Kelsey and Mary, were out of town on a work trip. He felt a little strange that Sydney would be over, and they would be spending time alone.

On their drive to Walmart, they listened to the news on the radio, *"As tensions grow between the US and China over the warships on the coast, NATO allies are coming in aid of the US, promising support in any conflict that could spark."*

"Warships on the coast?" Sydney asked.

"Yeah. They've been there for a week or so, no one really knows why."

The news was a little more than unsettling, and Parker switched channels. Getting onto the highway they ran into heavy traffic which was not all that uncommon for the time of day. He shrugged it off and looked at Sydney with a half smile. They sat in traffic for a while, jamming out to music while they waited.

Parker flipped his turn signal to switch into the exit lane and gunned the gas to get out in front of another car. The truck's engine shut off, leaving them to slow to a stop. Parker turned the key to the off position and back on, but nothing happened. He tried again, hoping it would work, but still nothing.

Could we have run out of gas. I don't recall having too much before we left, maybe waiting in the traffic drained it? Maybe?

"Start, why won't you?" Parker began to raise his voice.

He looked in his rearview mirror to see that the cars behind him were also sitting stuck in place. Other drivers looked just as confused, one even exiting the car and popping the hood.

"That's odd, it's not just us stuck here."

"That is weird, should we call someone?" Sydney asked, her voice filled with worry.

He pulled his phone from his pocket to dial, finding a black screen. "My phone won't turn on, will yours?"

Sydney, hers already in hand, shook her head saying, "Nope."

Parker looked around once more, noticing other people climbing out of their cars. *Maybe this is something happening all over? Did someone do something to everything in the area?*

"Let's get out and see if anyone knows what happened."

Sydney nodded and unlocked her door. They both climbed out and walked to the car just behind them. As they approached, the driver climbed out, but looked just as confused as they did.

"Any idea what happened?" Parker asked.

The man shook his head, "No, what could've just made all these cars stop dead in their tracks?"

"Beats me. Think it's the heat?"

"Nahh, it's been hotter."

Parker nodded and thanked the man. More troubled than he cared to admit, they returned to the truck.

Leaning against the hood because the heat was already too much inside the vehicle, he eyed the freeway.

People were starting to walk, and Parker said, "Well, I guess we should gather what we can and head to the house. I don't see it starting back up anytime soon."

But his mind wouldn't let go of it and kept circling the problem. *What could've just killed everything around here? All of the cars, all of the phones, what could've done it?* He had an idea but didn't want to think about it.

"So, what do you think happened? All of these cars stopped, and your phone won't work," Sydney asked.

"An EMP is my first thought," Parker replied, looking at the road ahead. "The fact that everything just shut off reminds me of the books."

"Well, we both know what happens after an EMP, and I don't want to be in the middle of it," Sydney exclaimed. "And if it is something else, and vehicles work again, we can come get the truck later."

"Agreed, let's get what we need and get out of here. Once we get back to the house, we can see if things work. We aren't too far," Parker said.

Parker opened the back door and lifted the seat. Under it he kept simple things he could need, tools, a few MREs, and a small medical kit. Between him and Sydney they had it all gathered up. Parker looked behind them and saw multiple groups of people gathering together and talking. They began down the off-ramp on their way home.

"Let's hope things don't get bad too fast, at least for a little while," Sydney said.

"Hopefully, but you know that won't happen," Parker said. The nagging feeling of just how bad this could be tickled his brain harder and harder with each passing moment.

They walked past the traffic light at the bottom of the off-ramp and towards the neighborhood, the roads littered with people standing near disabled cars. Parker was pressing his mind, trying to figure out why someone would target Nashville for an attack like this over somewhere like D.C. Nashville was just a poe dunk town. Aside from being the home of country music stars, they had nothing else to boast about.

"Hey, Parker," someone yelled out to them.

Parker looked around, trying to figure out who had called him when he spotted his friend. "Hey Leo, how'd you beat us home? We left at the same time."

"I took the back roads home instead of the highway, so I've been here for a while. Do you guys know what happened?"

"I'm not one hundred percent sure just yet, but my leading theory is an EMP. Where's your mom?"

"She went up to Clarksville to see her friends, they left while we were at lunch."

"Hope she can make it back safe."

Leo shrugged. "She probably won't be back for a couple of days. You know how she is, try to avoid any physical activity if she can."

Deep down Parker wondered if Leo knew what an EMP would mean. "We're going to go back to the house, but we need to talk a bit. We need to figure out a plan. I don't think this is temporary. Things are only going to get worse."

At first Leo's expression was shock, but quickly shifted, his head nodding. "Agreed. I'll come over there in a few minutes, I need to get some stuff out of my car."

They climbed the stairs to the porch and set everything down. Parker reached for his house key and jammed it into the lock. He carefully opened the door, making sure their dog, Nala, wasn't on the other side. He grabbed the stuff and brought it inside, dumping it onto the dining room table.

"Now what?" Sydney asked.

"Well, my mom and I used to camp a lot, so we have a butane stove we can cook on."

"That'll help," Sydney said, "I can do an inventory of all the food on hand."

Parker thought back to the first time he and Sydney chatted about being prepared. They first talked about books they'd read, then things they did. They were similar in thinking when it came to problems. They admired each other's preparedness for different situations. Both had survival kits in their cars, their backpacks, everywhere.

He paused and said, "Please. I want to know how long we have with the supplies on hand."

"Sure thing," Sydney said, spinning on her heel and heading to the kitchen.

Parker made his way to the basement and began looking through the shelves trying to find their camping supplies. A box labeled butane caught his eye, and he hoped the stove might be inside. He pulled it off of the shelf and opened the top, finding nothing but butane canisters. *Good to know we have quite a bit of that.*

He returned the box to the shelf and continued looking, finding a small bag about the size of the stove. He pulled it off of the shelf and unzipped it, happy when a stove was inside. He brought it upstairs and set it on the kitchen counter.

"How's it going?" He asked.

"Good, I've finished the cabinets, now the pantry."

"Alright, I dug the stove out, we need to go through everything in the fridge first, but we can at least warm whatever up."

"Good. Are you going to talk to Leo?"

Parker nodded, "Yeah, I'll go do that, and then we can figure out what's next."

Parker stepped outside and found Leo already making his way over. He stood for a moment on the porch gazing out at their neighborhood before heading down the driveway to meet him. "So, you've read the books about EMPs, right?"

"Yeah, I think so," Leo replied.

"Well, in almost every single one of them, everyone goes crazy when they run out of food. Or just because there is no more power or electronics. We need to keep ourselves safe somehow," Parker explained.

"What do you suggest?" Leo asked.

"Does your mom still have that old car?" Parker questioned.

"Yeah, why?" Leo asked, "It won't run; no other car does."

"Because if it works, we can make a grocery store

run. The best thing we can do is get ahead of the crowds and take advantage of this time and hope no one else catches on."

They walked back over to Leo's house and went inside; Parker waited by the front door for Leo to get the keys. Coming back out, the key ring swinging on his finger, he strutted over to the car.

Hopping into the driver's seat he said, "Here goes nothing." He cranked the ignition and the engine hummed to life. "Yes!" He exclaimed, pumping his fist in the air.

"Good, turn it off so we can save gas." Parker told him, "We can use that and go get food from the grocery store, but we need to go soon."

"Alright, let me empty the backseat and trunk so we have all the room we need," Leo said.

"Meet me at my house when you're done," Parker said.

Parker went back to the house and went inside to find
Sydney coming out of the pantry. She shut the door and set the notebook on the counter. "Done?"

"Yep, I need a break," she said, going to the living room.

"Do that. Leo and I are going to the grocery store to get some food. Stock up before it all runs out," Parker explained.

"Okay, do you want me to come with you guys?"

"You don't have to. I think we'll be good on our own. He's cleaning out his mom's old car so we can head over there and get as much as possible."

"Okay," she said, "I'll hang out here with Nala."

Parker made his way to his mom's bedroom and looked around in the closet, eventually finding the gun safe with the key resting on top. He opened it up and grabbed out two pistols with holsters. Also, inside was some cash, and he quickly pocketed it. After relocking the safe, he returned downstairs and looked at Sydney.

"Be safe," she said with a smile.

"I will," Parker said.

He climbed into the car and set the second pistol on the center console. "Here, just in case things get bad."

"Thanks. Do you really think things will go south?"

Parker shrugged. "The hope is it doesn't."

Leo drove through the lot for a minute before parking. It was riddled with abandoned cars. He parked in a spot, hoping the car would blend in. Inside there were few people left, just employees, everyone else likely left and went home.

"Hey, sorry but we are only taking cash for anything bought, the power outage messed stuff up," the door greeter explained.

"That's okay, we brought some. Thanks for the warning." Parker responded, grabbing them each a cart.

They strolled the aisles at a fast pace, grabbing anything that caught their eye, mostly keeping to canned goods that would store for longer. As they neared the produce section, they grabbed what they could, knowing fresh produce would only be available for a week until they could grow more.

Once they were satisfied with their haul, they brought everything up to the front and to a register. One employee manned the whole checkout section.

"Are you sure you guys need all of that?" The clerk asked.

"Yes, we're sure. Why?"

"It's going to take me a while to add it all up without a scanner." He looked at them side eyed and then back to the items they'd chosen. "That's a lotta stuff," the clerk said.

"Graduation party, man," Leo held up his hands with his middle and ring finger down for a party time symbol. "Well, that and my mom made me grab some other stuff."

"Mmmhm," the man said, eyeing them but tallying up the items.

While they waited for the man to count everything up and write it down, they moved off to the side and quietly talked about what could be next.

"It's hard to say what will happen, could be anything. Maybe people go insane, or maybe we learn to work together as a society."

"I guess there is no telling what could happen," Leo said.

The clerk waved them back to the counter. "Excuse me. The total is three hundred fifty-two dollars even."

Parker nodded and started digging into his wallet. He grabbed out the exact amount the man was asking, handing it over.

He counted it before shoving it into a pocket on his ugly grocery store apron. "Have a good one, be safe out there."

They both nodded, taking their carts outside to load into the car. Leo took a minute to glance around the parking lot before unlocking the trunk. "All this makes me nervous."

"Yeah, me too. Let's get going," Parker said, placing the last bag in the back seat.

Once back on the road home, Parker said, "That was an easy enough trip, now we need to get going on other things to help move forward."

Chapter 2

Kelsey Davidson

Near Everett, Washington

Kelsey squinted as the sunlight gleamed into the window. She forced herself to sit up and wake up before walking over to the coffee pot. All she needed to do was hit the button, and poor tasting motivational coffee would come pouring out. As much as she hated hotel coffee, it always made her days easier.

While she waited for the coffee to brew, she peered around the room at the "art" that filled the walls. *How could they call this stuff art? It's a bunch of lines and paint splatters.*

When she heard the ding of the coffee maker, her head perked up, excited to get the little joy her day would bring. She took a deep breath after the first sip and forced herself to get dressed. Her job wasn't hard by any means, it was just mentally taxing, making it hard for her to get out of bed every morning. She just couldn't turn down the pay she got, though.

She took the last swig of coffee before setting the cup on the counter and heading out of the room. She heard the loud click of the door shutting as she walked down the hall to the front desk. Being on the first floor, all she heard over the night was cars driving by on the highway.

Not a soul in sight, apparently the world was dead at four in the morning. She wandered the parking lot looking for an unfamiliar car, one of the hardest parts of going out of town. When she found it she was finally able to head to work and get it over with.

As she pulled up to the gate of the base the MP reached his hand out, awaiting her ID. She handed the card over and waited for him to let her through.

"Alright ma'am you're good to go, have a good one."

"Thank you. You, too," she said as the arm raised.

She pulled away and began her navigation to the site for their research. Kelsey was part of a company that offered private security for research operations nationwide. Almost every month out of the year she was in a new place for work. Kelsey had been in Washington for almost a week now, missing her son's last day of school. Her trip was supposed to last another week, maybe longer.

As she pulled into the makeshift parking lot, she found it was nearly full. She parked in one of the only empty spaces and made her way over to her security office. She walked in for the first time and just like every other site she'd been on, found a small, cramped room full of computers and screens. *What's new?*

She dropped her stuff off in the room before heading back outside to find her team. She found them all gathered around a small tent, covering a map of the area. It was mostly woods, the only clearing in the middle where they were. There were colored pins lining the perimeter of the site, along with a few marking locations. She pointed to one of the pins, "Group A, you guys will start here, and B, you'll be here."

Everyone nodded and headed out to their patrol locations. She waited for them all to disperse before heading back into the office. Her eyes adjusted to the bright screens illuminating the room. She sat in the hardback chair and navigated the screens, looking around at the different available cameras and pages preloaded onto the monitors. The wall above her was covered with what seemed like a hundred screens, all showing different feeds, radio transcripts from her teams, and a map of the area.

Once she was done looking through everything, she leaned back, watching. It was a quiet first day. Usually, she had a ton of meetings with the people doing the research, but her boss had taken care of all of it. She kicked her feet up and stared at the cameras, her eyes bouncing from screen to screen. As the sun came up, some of the cameras got a bad glare, making them impossible to look at.

After looking at the cameras for what felt like forever and seeing nothing but her people patrolling, she eventually gave up and decided to take her lunch break. She got out of the chair, her legs half asleep and her back aching. She stretched before exiting the cramped room. The amount of equipment inside kept it feeling very full and hot from the heat the machines emitted.

Outside she found the tents that had their food set up under it. Each day they ordered something new from a restaurant around the area, enough for both shifts of people. They kept it all on warmers throughout the day, so it eventually developed a weird taste if it sat long enough.

She made herself a plate of food. Today it was pasta and a few simple pizzas. With her plate, she returned to the office. Opening the door, she hadn't been met with the glow of monitors, or hum of electronics. She thought maybe she had hit the switch on her way out. Nope, it was still flipped to the on position.

What in the world? The switch is still on, what happened?

She stepped back outside of the office and took a bite of her food on her way to her boss' office. She knocked, and received no response. She looked around hoping he was outside somewhere.

"Why isn't my phone working!" he yelled from the parking lot.

"Hey, what's going on? Is it an outage?" Kelsey questioned, running over at the sound of his voice.

"I think so, but my phone is dead. Can I use yours to call the power company?"

"Sure thing."

Kelsey juggled her plate and fork before grabbing her phone and handing it to him.

"Ugh, it's not working either."

"I swear it was charged a few minutes ago."

Kelsey took the phone back and tested it herself. He was right. She took another bite of food and waited as he thought.

"Could this be something with those ships? Did they mess something up?"

"I mean, it's feasible, but why would they do it?"

~

Kelsey looked around for one of the patrol teams. They had no way to contact them as all the radios were out. She needed to inform them of what was going on so they could keep an eye out for anything that could threaten the research. *Is someone trying to make a move on the base? Took out communications in the area so they could have an opening?*

She found one of the teams after a while of searching. "Hey, we have a problem on our hands. Power is out and so are the radios."

The group gave her a shocked look, "Do you have any idea what happened?"

"No, not yet. We are working on it, but for now we need you guys on high alert. There is a chance this happened so someone could infiltrate the area."

"Will do."

"Thank you. I'll come find you if I find anything else out."

Kelsey returned to the main camp and looked around, but not much was going on, mostly people standing around not knowing what to do. She returned to the security office, hoping the power was back, and everything was fixed. Nope.

"What could this be? Power, radios, phones, they don't all just go out. Not like this."

"Kelsey," her boss called from behind her. "Did you relay what you could to the patrol teams?"

"I did to one of the teams, they'll eventually cross

paths with another so they'll all know about it soon. In the meantime, have you figured out what could've happened?"

"Yes and no. My first thought is an EMP. The thing I don't know is if it was local, or nationwide. There is no way to know without leaving and traveling around."

"An EMP is the only thing that could've done this, but I agree, we have no way to know local or country wide. If it is country wide, then I need to get home."

"Why? We still have a job to do. There is sensitive information locked behind some of these doors. We at least need to stay on post until we get orders from the higher ups."

"If this is country wide, then my son is across the country, alone. People won't wait to go crazy; he's not staying alone for too long."

Her boss thought. "Wait a little bit at least, if we don't hear anything in an hour or two, you can go. I can get by with Mary. We can probably figure it out without you."

"Thank you."

Her current worry was how long it would take for her to get back to Nashville. She knew it would be a long journey, but it had to be done to make sure he was safe.

What is going to be the best way? I wrote down the times for a few routes since I thought about driving up, but how much do I multiply it to account for walking and taking breaks? I can at least get an idea.

She grabbed her notebook out of the backpack sitting in the office, though she couldn't read it in the dark room. She brought it outside and flipped to the page where everything was written down. Regardless of which way she went, it would take weeks. *I'm in for a long hard workout.*

~

"Alright Kelsey, I guess this is goodbye. Oh, wait," her boss began before running off to the security office.

He returned a minute later with a black case in hand. "What's that?"

"It's a radio with an antenna, it should still work, the case is a type of faraday cage. Use this to get in contact when you reach home, let us know how the rest of the US is."

Kelsey took the case, "Thank you, I will."

"Stay safe out there, get back to your boy."

She still had a few things to grab from her car, so she made her way in the direction of the parking lot. She hit the unlock button on the fob, reached for the handle and realized the car was still locked. She pulled the key back from her pocket and stuck it into the handle, twisting to unlock the door.

She grabbed the small lunchbox she kept with snacks out of the backseat. She dumped the contents into her backpack, then shoved the radio case in. She shut the door and continued down the dirt path to leave the base. It took her only a few minutes to get back to pavement, though it was a few miles to get off of base.

~

Once Kelsey got off the base, she could see it was nearing sunset. She stopped for a few minutes and caught her breath. She hadn't walked this much since last fall when she was taking daily walks. It was only about to get worse.

She followed the road for another couple of minutes before reaching an on-ramp for Highway 5; it was littered with cars. Most of the people seem to have abandoned them in favor of getting home. Upon reaching the top of the onramp, she heard people yelling at each other. She walked over to one of the groups and could hear a woman yelling at a man, "How is this my fault? You were driving."

"You've always hated me. We're done," the man said, walking away.

She walked over to the woman. "What's going on?"

"Well, we were driving on the highway when every car slowed to a roll. He tried to fix the car, but nothing happened. That's when he started blaming me for it. He somehow thinks this is my fault."

"There's no way for this to be anyone's fault."

"Everyone out here on the highway is going crazy. No one knows what happened. Do you know what happened?"

"I'm still not quite sure. All I know is that I need to get home."

"Where are you from?"

"Well, I'm coming from the base out here, and I'm going to Tennessee," she explained. "I was here on a work trip."

"That's a long way to go. I wish you luck on your journey."

"Thank you, you, too."

She walked past groups of angry people trying to get

home after work. She tried her best to ignore them before a woman stopped her, she was visibly concerned.

"Can I help you?"

"Some guys just tried to steal some stuff from me. I don't know where they went."

"What do you want me to do about it? I'm trying to get home."

"Where are you going?"

"Tennessee, why?"

"Can I travel with you? I can give you some food and help you along the journey."

"Sure, but you better not slow me down."

The woman nodded. "So, what's your name?"

"Kelsey, yours?"

"Anna. Thank you for helping me."

They began walking down the highway as it got dark. They waited until they were away from most of the crowds before walking off the highway to set up camp for the night. Kelsey set her things down, sat and used her backpack as a pillow.

"What do we sleep on?" Anna asked.

"What do you mean? We sleep on the ground. Haven't you ever been camping?"

"No. I've always found camping boring."

"O... okay," Kelsey said, setting her backpack at the base of a tree. *I'm biting off more than I can chew letting her come with me. It's okay though, it might be nice to have some company.*

Anna looked around and eventually set her backpack

against a tree. She looked over at Kelsey and copied her, leaning on a tree. Kelsey watched Anna struggle to get comfortable.

~

The following day, Kelsey woke up to Anna screaming.

"What are you doing? We are going to get found."

"There were ants crawling on my legs."

"So? They don't bite," Kelsey replied. "Your screaming will cause people to come over here, and I don't want anyone over here."

"Alright, calm down. What's so bad about people anyway?" Anna asked, picking up her backpack so they could start walking.

"Two women, alone, without any form of protection. You tell me."

"I don't think that's a problem, but whatever you say."

Kelsey stretched, her back ached from sleeping on the ground, something she would have to get used to. Once she was all stretched and most of the way awake, she was ready to hit the road.

Kelsey picked up her pack and hoisted it over her shoulder. They hiked up the hill and started walking along the highway. The air was still and silent until they reached the top of a hill and could see a woman trying to fight off two men. Kelsey led them off the highway a little so they could see what was going on and be hidden behind some bushes.

They listened as the woman yelled at the men,

followed by some screaming. The screaming stopped as the men ran away, holding her purse and some cash.

"That is what's wrong with people." Kelsey looked over at Anna. She got up and returned to the road. Shortly after, Anna followed her. They walked over to the woman and asked what had happened.

"Well, I was about to start walking home because I finally gave up on my car working, and those two guys came over and stole my purse."

"I wish there were something we could do for you," Kelsey said. "But we have to get home."

"What do you mean? Why don't we help get her purse back?" Anna whispered in Kelsey's ear.

"Are you kidding me? You want to take on two grown men without any form of weapons?" Kelsey whispered back to Anna, anger in her voice.

"I think we at least need to help her."

"Not happening. I'm sorry, but I don't think it will end well."

"Fine, but I think we are doing the wrong thing."

"I'm sorry, but we need to go. We wish you luck."

Kelsey and Anna continued down the road, passing abandoned cars. They walked mostly in silence, aside from the occasional bird chirping. Kelsey stopped when she saw a map by the side of the road, taking a minute to examine it and find where they were. They were just north of Seattle, probably only a few miles.

"Think we can make it to Seattle soon?"

"Maybe, how far are we?" Anna asked.

"Umm, looks like we're about three miles, give or

take," Kelsey said.

"That's a long way to go."

"Well, to make it to Nashville, where I need to be, we need to go about twenty-five hundred miles."

"Whoa, that is much further. Don't you have to go to Georgia with me and help me make it?"

"What ever made you think I'm going to Georgia with you?"

"Well, I thought you were going with me, you know, so I actually make it and don't run into trouble," Anna said, "You seem to know a lot more about all this stuff than I do..."

"No. I am not going an additional, I don't know, hundred miles just to turn right around and go back to Tennessee," Kelsey exclaimed. "By the time we are in Nashville, you should be comfortable enough to finish the trek yourself."

Anna grumbled, "Fine."

Kelsey wished she hadn't invited Anna to join her. It hadn't even been twenty-four hours, and she was already on her nerves. She hoped it would get better, though she doubted it would.

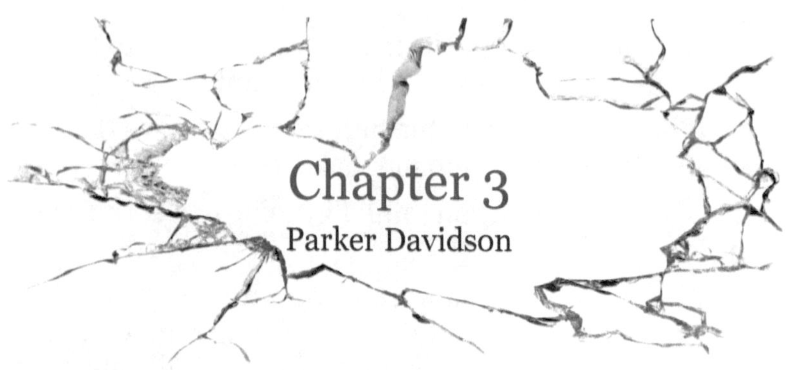

Chapter 3
Parker Davidson

When Parker and Leo got back to the house, Leo helped Parker get everything inside. Once it was all in the kitchen, Leo left to go do his own thing.

"I'm back," Parker yelled through the house.

"Welcome back, how'd it go?" Sydney asked.

"Good, we got enough food for a long time. Most of it won't ever go bad, but we did get some produce and bread that we need to use pretty quick. Figured it'd be nice to have one last time."

"Did you get dog food for Nala?"

"Yes, I grabbed all the bags of her current food and all of the bags of another brand that's mostly the same," Parker replied.

"Okay. I'll help you put everything away," Sydney said, getting up from the couch.

Parker grabbed the bags of dog food and carried them downstairs, setting them by one on the shelves. As they put things away, Sydney wrote it all on the list, wanting to keep track.

With everything put away, they needed a break. Parker sat in the living room and read for a little bit, occupying his mind for long enough to rest.

Sydney awoke a few hours later, while Parker was reading his book. "How long was I out?"

"A few hours, want to help me get dinner going?"

"Sure, are we using the meat in the fridge?"

"Yes, I want to use everything we can in the fridge before it goes bad. We probably have a few days before it is ruined, so we have some time."

Parker grabbed the ground beef that was thawing the day before out of the fridge and set it on the counter. While it sat, he unzipped the bag that held the butane stove and began setting it up. He threw the bag away, figuring it wouldn't get put away for a long time.

"What do we need to do next? We have more food now, so we need to do more to help prepare us right?"

"I'm not quite sure yet. What comes to mind right away is water. The couple of cases we got, and what we already have, will last a month, maybe two if we stretch it. But without AC, and it being mid-summer, we shouldn't ration it. The best way for us to get more would be rain collection, but we would need to boil it to make sure it is safe to drink. The other way is finding a creek in the woods down the road and getting some that way."

Parker had only walked through the woods bordering the neighborhood a few times before. Though, on one of his walks, he distinctly remembered a creek somewhere in the forest.

Sydney nodded. "Well, once we get to the point of not having enough, we can figure it out."

They both made bowls of leftover spaghetti before

heading to the dining room, eating in silence. When Parker finished he returned to the kitchen, trying to figure out how to clean the bowl. He grabbed a water bottle from the counter and poured it in, getting all of the sauce off. Sydney brought hers in and set it on the counter for him.

He set the bowls on the counter on a towel to dry while he fed Nala; Sydney went into the living room and sat on the couch to relax. After Nala finished eating, Parker let her outside and back in, making sure to lock the back door.

How long will it take to rebuild? Months? There is quite a bit to be done, but allies of the US would surely come help. Right?

"Ready to go to bed?" Sydney asked from the living room, getting up to make her way to the guest room.

Parker returned to reality. "Sure, I'm tired. It's been a day."

~

The following morning, Parker fumbled his way through making stovetop coffee, something he'd never done before. He had hoped the package of instant coffee had some level of instructions, but he was wrong. He guessed that he was supposed to boil the water then pour the coffee in, hoping that was right.

He pulled the pot from the stove and let it sit for a minute before pouring some into his cup. He brought the cup to his mouth and took a sip, almost wanting to spit it out for how bad it was, though he didn't. *This is better than no coffee. Just drink it and you'll get used to it. It's not THAT bad.*

He took another sip and winced at the poor taste

before setting his cup on the counter to let Nala in from outside. He gave her a treat, and returned to the kitchen.

Nala came running into the room with a toy in her mouth. She dropped it right in front of him and sat down. He picked the toy up and threw it into the dining room; immediately she chased after it.

It's great that animals would never know things like an EMP happened. The little joy she brings lightens everything up.

Sydney came stumbling into the kitchen yawning. "Morning, how long have you been up?"

Parker turned to see her standing in the doorway. "Not too long. Made some okay coffee."

"What's on the agenda today?"

"Well, we could go into town and see how things are. It's probably bad, but I want to get some more supplies from the store. I haven't heard much, so maybe it's not too bad. We'll have to see. And if it's bad, then we can just come back."

"Alright, well, let's go soon before most people get up. If no one was crazy last night they likely will be today."

Sydney went back to the bedroom and got dressed. Meanwhile, Parker threw the toy one last time for Nala before heading to do the same. Once he was dressed, he grabbed his pistol and pocketknife. He grabbed his wallet, figuring he wouldn't need it, but wanted to have it just in case. He went upstairs to his mom's bedroom and opened the gun safe. He grabbed another pistol out and took it downstairs for Sydney.

"Be good, Nala. Don't let anyone break in while we are gone," he called inside before shutting the door.

They walked down the street and out of the neighborhood, immediately seeing the grocery store. They walked over to its parking lot which was surrounded by tons of other buildings. They saw a group of people by one of the fast food places and quickly turned to walk the other way to avoid the group, not wanting a confrontation, though the area was relatively quiet.

After seeing the state of the area, they decided to head back to the house and make a plan for what would be next.

"Well, we need to try to stockpile cash and coins so we can get things when we need them. You know, take advantage of cash still being used."

"I almost wonder if we can get all of our friends who live nearby to help us with creating a group," Parker exclaimed.

"What do you mean, create a group?"

"Well, we can't do this alone, especially if our parents won't be home for at least a month. If we can make a group of people we trust, then we have people who we can help and who can help us."

"Ah, that could be great. It would make life a lot easier if we didn't have to do everything and could split it among other people."

"And, if anything is to happen, we have a group to help us fight anyone who tries to come after us. Safety in numbers."

Chapter 4
Kelsey Davidson

Seattle, Washington

The duo caught a glimpse of the fading welcome sign to Seattle as they passed it, the city's skyline coming into view as they reached the top of a hill.

"Almost there. Listen, Anna, I need you to pay attention to your surroundings while we are here. Please."

Anna just a couple steps behind her shrugged. "I think it'll be okay."

Kelsey clenched her fist lightly. "Then you don't know what Seattle is like. Just remember I can leave you here."

"Whatever," Anna said, an almost teenage angst filling her voice.

Their journey up to this point had already proved a test of patience for Kelsey. The blind trust Anna instilled in society and others to keep her safe needed to end. Kelsey, for her whole life, had always read situations before they got a chance to go south, but Anna needed to learn some things.

As they delved deeper into the city, they found tons of people running in and out of stores, most coming out of the nearby grocery store with carts full of canned goods, blankets, and water bottles. Other people were fighting in alley ways.

Kelsey patted her pocket, feeling the welcoming presence of her pocketknife. *We need to get out of here before I have to use this. That is the absolute last thing I want to do.*

As the sun dipped below the tallest buildings, Kelsey knew they needed to move fast. "Let's hurry out of here so we can find somewhere to sleep."

Anna nodded, "Works for me."

Kelsey barely even heard her, her mind focusing on getting them out of the city. Once they were nearing the outskirts they began looking for somewhere to hunker down for the night. Between the ditches off of the road of the open farm land, there was nowhere they'd be out of sight. Though they did eventually find a dense grove of evergreens to settle into.

They slipped off of the road and walked into the grove for a couple minutes before stopping for the day. Kelsey shrugged her backpack off and sat down.

"I see what you mean about Seattle, I always thought it was... better than that."

Kelsey nodded. "The city's been on the edge for years, the EMP just pushed it off."

Kelsey ripped open her backpack and grabbed out two granola bars, tossing one to Anna. "Before I came for vacation, social media always made it look better."

"Can't trust the internet."

~

The next morning Kelsey jolted awake from Anna shaking her. She rubbed her eyes at the bright morning dawn, "What?"

"Couldn't sleep any longer so I figured we could get an early start," Anna said, her voice filled with energy.

Kelsey stretched, all of her joints popping. "We need to keep a steady pace today. We're about two hundred miles from Oregon; I want to be there in a few days."

"That's... a lot."

"Well, maybe we can find a working car and give our legs a break for a little while. If not... we keep walking."

After a quick breakfast they got on the road, the morning mist making the air feel thick. They walked in silence, listening to the chirps of birds, each lost in their own thoughts.

"So, how long have you lived in Nashville?" Anna asked, kicking an empty bottle.

Kelsey brought herself back to reality. "Um, since my son was born, so just under eighteen years. Where do you call home?"

"I live in a small town off the highway just south of the Tennessee border. My whole family lives there so it's nice."

"Sounds nice." Kelsey said, her eyes tracking movement down the hill ahead. "We got people up ahead."

Kelsey watched the group of three growing closer with each step. Kelsey was weary of approaching, not knowing if they were good or bad. She'd heard her fair share of stories, always praying it would never happen to her.

One of the people waved. "Hello, how are you guys?"

"We're good, trying to get home. You guys?"

"Same here. How far are you guys?"

"Two thousand miles, trying to get across the country. How about you guys?"

"Just trying to get to Vancouver, so not too far. Maybe we can make it soon. We heard from another group about warships on the coast, do you know anything about it?"

"No, I haven't heard anything about it. What do you think they're doing?" Anna asked.

One of the women chimed in, "That group said they thought they were the ones to launch the EMP."

Kelsey thought, *Possible, sure.* "Well, good luck."

"Same to you, too. Get home safe."

Kelsey nodded. "These warships have been on the news all week, how have you not heard about them?"

"Simple, I don't watch the news. It's full of fake news anyway, so how do you know what's real and what's fake?"

"I mean, you got a point there. I still watch it for the grain of salt that I can take from it. But, if they're back, and if they did launch the EMPs, then maybe it's an invasion."

Anna stopped, her face paling. "What?"

"It's okay, we still have enough of a military and people who want to protect the US, and I'm also sure that NATO or someone will come in if it is needed."

After a little while they found themselves reaching the top of another hill. This time, there was a bigger group gathered around a beat-up white van at the bottom. The road ahead of it was filled with abandoned cars, and a few people wandering between the traffic.

Kelsey reached her arm out to stop Anna. "Let's wait a minute and see what this is about."

They watched. The group was just talking with one another. Seemed safe enough. They descended the hill and approached the group. "How's it going?"

"It was good until we reached this traffic jam. We heard about the EMP. The van still runs, so I'm going to take people out east as far as we can."

"What were you guys doing out here?"

"Oh, it's an airport shuttle for Seattle International. We were on the way to one of our drop off spots further south, but we got stuck in the traffic. Turns out, it isn't going to end anytime soon. Anyways. Where are you guys heading?"

Kelsey shook her head. "You can't get us two thousand miles, but you can get us closer."

"Oh, wow, where are you from?"

"Tennessee."

The driver nodded his head. "I see. Well, I'm happy to give you a ride for as long as I can."

"Thank you, we appreciate it."

Everyone loaded into the van, and they were off. They were forced to drive on the shoulder to avoid the stalled-out cars.

Kelsey could see smoke filling the air up ahead,

coming from an open field. "What's that?"

"Looks like a downed plane. Must've just taken off when the EMP hit. Hope some people survived."

After they passed the traffic, and they were back on the pavement, Kelsey reached into her backpack, grabbing a tattered paperback. It was a survival guide she always kept in her backpack, never knowing when she would need it.

Chapter 5
Kelsey Davidson

Baker City, Oregon

Kelsey was woken up when the van rattled to a stop, and the door slid open. The sun was setting, still just above the horizon. She rubbed her eyes. "Where are we?"

"Near the Idaho-Oregon border," the driver said from the back, tossing a backpack to one of the people.

"How much further do you think we can get?"

"Hundred more miles, give or take. It doesn't get the greatest mileage, but it was full before the traffic back there," he responded, sitting back in the squeaky driver's seat.

She shifted in her seat as he took off, racing down the road. She grabbed her book off of the floor and looked for her place. After two pages, the van lurched to a stop, her head hitting the back of the seat in front of her. She dropped the book and looked at the road ahead, seeing two people behind cars, guns drawn. One of the men pointed a gun right at the van.

"Get down!" Kelsey yelled as the sound of shattering glass filled the air followed by a thud.

Kelsey looked up to see the driver's body slumped over the steering wheel, a giant hole in the headrest, and Anna covered in crimson. Another bullet flew, though this time, it wasn't at them. She looked at the roadblock and found one of the two people slumped over the hood of a car.

She wrapped her hand around the door handle, debating whether or not she should get out. She pulled open the door and got out, crouching behind it. She looked around the door to see the surviving man walking over.

"Are you guys okay?" he asked, walking around the door.

Kelsey took a sigh of relief before standing up. "Almost all of us are." She looked back at the driver. "Back to walking."

"I'm sorry you guys got caught in that. I was looting that car, and he came out of nowhere demanding my stuff. It spiraled out of control pretty fast."

Kelsey shook her head. "God, it's only been three days since the EMP, and people are already killing each other over scraps."

"I know," he said, walking over to the man's body, grabbing the rifle out of his hand, and the pistol off his hip. He reached the pistol out to Kelsey. "Here, you'll need this."

She nodded, wrapping her hands around the cold metal grip. "Thanks."

He dug into the backpack on the man's back and pulled out a spare magazine and a box of ammo, handing them over to Kelsey. She shoved them in her pocket for now, walking back over to the van where Anna was standing just outside of it.

She brushed past her and grabbed her backpack, putting the gun and ammo inside, switching it for a water bottle. "Here, go wash off. I'll get your stuff out."

She took the water bottle and went to the ditch to wash the blood off of her. Meanwhile, Kelsey reached in and grabbed Anna's backpack out of the back, rejoining her. She waited for her to finish, though the blood never stopped streaming down her face.

She took the water bottle from Anna and looked at her forehead. The bullet had grazed her just enough to cause her to bleed.

"Here, sit down for me," she said calmly, trying to keep her from freaking out.

She dug into her backpack for the makeshift first aid kit she had made before her trip. She ripped it open and looked for the roll of gauze, using it to cover the wound on Anna's head.

"What happened? Am I okay?"

"Yes. The bullet grazed you, you'll be fine."

She could hear Anna breathing a bit heavier. "You're fine. It's okay, just a small cut. But since it's your head, it bleeds like crazy."

Anna calmed down a bit. "Okay. I trust you."

Kelsey wrapped the gauze on her head, using a small strip of medical tape to hold it in place. "There, all done."

The man walked back over to them. "You alright?"

"She'll be fine, the bullet barely grazed her."

"Well, glad you're okay. I should head out, my wife and daughter are probably worried sick about me."

"I'm sure they are. We should probably get walking, too. Thank you for the gun."

"For sure. I already have one, so I figured that could help you in your journey."

Anna had finally gotten up from the roadside, walking over to Kelsey. "Got any painkillers in that kit?"

"I think so. I'm sure your head hurts pretty bad."

Anna nodded lightly, taking the pill Kelsey handed her. She used the rest of the water to take it before they set off. They only had an hour at most before the sun would set below the horizon. Kelsey wanted to stop before then, though. They needed to get away from the van and the attention it would bring.

Once they were a decent way from the van, they found a few trees they could hide in for the night. Kelsey sat against a tree and pulled out a couple of beef sticks, handing two to Anna. "How are you feeling?"

"The pain is going away a bit, but not much. Hopefully, sleeping will help."

Kelsey nodded. "It will. We'll replace your bandage in the morning before we start walking."

"Question. Could we find a doctor in the next town to make sure I'm okay?"

Kelsey shook her head. "No. Towns are the last thing we need right now. You'll be fine. It was a little graze, nothing crazy."

"Come on, Kelsey," Anna snapped. "Please."

"No. I already told you, you'll be fine. I promise," Kelsey calmly explained, trying not to yell at Anna.

"Fine. But when I die, I'll blame you."

Anna slumped on the tree, beginning to get tired, while Kelsey focused on getting a fire going. She needed Anna to understand where she was coming from on most of these things if she ever wanted to survive until Nashville.

She wandered into the forest in search of kindling for a small fire, at least enough to warm up some dehydrated food she had with her.

She returned momentarily with an armfull of sticks, ready to make a fire. She peered over to Anna, who was flipping through a magazine.

"Want some chili?"

Anna nodded. Once it was done, Kelsey handed her the bag, and they ate in silence.

~

Parker Davidson

Parker stood up from the couch as a knock on the door echoed through the room. He pulled it open, shocked to find Leo at the door, his face etched with concern.

Parker leaned on the doorframe. "What's up man?"

"Went into town today and found there was a giant group of people gathered. No idea what it was."

"We saw the same thing yesterday, though it wasn't a huge group."

"I hope it isn't something bad," Leo began, pausing as some yelling was heard in the distance. "But the only way to find out is to go."

"We'll try to go tomorrow and see what's up."

"Perfect, let me know what you guys find out. I need to get back, told myself I needed to organize the garage to make things easy to find."

Parker laughed. "I need to do the same thing, but not today. I'm going to try to get some seeds in the ground."

Leo waved as Parker shut the door. He returned to the living room to find Sydney on the couch, and Nala chasing her tail.

"That's weird."

"What?" Parker asked, flopping onto the couch.

"What Leo was talking about, about the group of people."

"Oh, yeah, maybe we can find out what it is about tomorrow."

"We can do that. What's the plan for today?"

"Well, I want to get some seeds in the ground so we can start growing fresh food. I'm sure canned food will get boring soon. And maybe we could talk to some neighbors and see what's going on."

"Alright, well, I can talk to neighbors if you want; I don't know much about gardening or any of that," Sydney exclaimed.

"I'll teach you, don't worry. It's not super hard, just tedious."

Parker went into the kitchen and grabbed the seed packets from the counter–tomatoes, carrots, and green beans, all left over from last season. Outside, he knelt next to the garden bed, which usually had flowers this time of year. Now it was needed for survival. He worked the soil, loosening it up before dropping seeds into it.

Once all of the seeds were planted, he grew curious if the hose still had some water in the lines. He found the spigot on the side of the house and slowly turned it, a minute later a weak stream trickled out. He watered the seeds before filling three buckets from the garage with the leftover water.

His mind jumped to their water supply, they had enough water bottles for now, but when they ran out and the pipes ran dry they'd be in trouble. An idea popped into his head. He walked around the house counting gutter ends, planting an empty bucket beneath each. He looked across the street to see Sydney talking with a neighbor. Her gestures suggested a lively conversation.

He returned to the garage and made sure they would have enough buckets to replace the others once they were full. He went inside, which was slightly cooler than outside, finding Nala waiting by the back door to go outside. He let her out before grabbing a handful of crackers out of the box on the counter. Parker settled down on the bench on the front porch, popping a cracker into his mouth as Sydney came back.

"How'd that go?"

"Most of everyone says they're okay without help," she began, wiping a bead of sweat from her brow. "From what I heard, the meeting was from the mayor, talking about his plan to keep peace in the town and try to keep cash in use."

Parker's face showed a growing shock. "What if we don't have cash? What then?"

Sydney frowned. "Not sure. Though they are doing meetings daily for the whole week."

Parker nodded, his gaze drifting to the empty, quiet streets. With the world unraveling, information was almost more important than food or water. Knowing as much as you could was a lifeline. Luckily, tomorrow they would learn more about the situation wiping out the US.

Chapter 6
Kelsey Davidson

Just east of Baker City, Oregon

The chittering of squirrels in the pine branches above pulled Kelsey from a restless sleep. She sat up, her back stiff from the hard ground, and glanced at Anna, who lay curled against the boulder, her chest rising and falling unevenly. The bandage on Anna's forehead was stained dark with blood; the outer layers soaked through. Kelsey's stomach tightened, and she was running low on supplies. She reached for her backpack, pulling out the first aid kit and gathering fresh gauze, tape, and antiseptic.

Crawling closer, she gently shook Anna's shoulder. No response. She shook harder, and Anna's eyes fluttered open, only to squint shut against the piercing morning sun.

"Hey, wake up," Kelsey said softly. "I need to change your bandage."

"Wh... what?" Anna mumbled, her voice thick with grogginess.

"You need to stay awake for this," Kelsey repeated, keeping her tone calm but firm. She worked quickly, peeling away the bloodied gauze to reveal the raw wound beneath. It wasn't festering, thank God, but it still oozed. She cleaned it with antiseptic, wincing as Anna hissed in pain, and applied fresh gauze, securing it with tape. "This should hold for now, but we're almost out of supplies. We need to make serious ground today."

Anna nodded weakly, her face pale. "I'll try."

Kelsey packed up the kit, her mind racing. Three days into their cross-country trek, and they'd barely covered a fraction of the two-thousand-plus miles to Nashville. Her goal was to be home by the end of the second week of the EMP—a near-impossible feat, but she clung to it like a lifeline. If they kept a steady pace, they might just make it.

They broke camp, slinging their backpacks over their shoulders, and hit the highway. The air was crisp, the road flanked by golden fields stretching toward the Idaho border. After a few minutes, the distant crack of gunfire echoed from a small town ahead. Kelsey froze, her hand instinctively brushing the pistol tucked into her waistband.

"We need to be careful," she said, her voice low. "That doesn't sound... friendly."

Anna frowned, adjusting her pack. "Friendly? Those were gunshots, Kelsey. You call that friendly?"

Kelsey shot her a dry look. "Sarcasm, Anna."

"Oh." Anna's lips twitched, but her eyes stayed fixed on the road, where the first buildings of the town came into view—squat, weathered structures under a gray sky. More gunshots rang out, sporadic now, like the last gasps of a fading storm.

As they neared the town's edge, a figure sprinted

from a building, clutching a bag and glancing wildly over their shoulder. No one followed, but the runner ducked behind a dumpster, out of sight. Kelsey's grip on her pistol tightened. "We can go around the town," she offered. "It'll take longer, but it's safer."

Anna shook her head, her jaw set despite the pain etched on her face. "No, let's go through. I know you want to get home, and so do I. The faster, the better."

Kelsey hesitated, then nodded. "Alright. Stay sharp."

They rounded a corner, stepping into the town's main square. The first few minutes were quiet, the streets eerily empty outside of the occasional abandoned car. But as they approached the center, chaos erupted. A grocery store loomed ahead, its parking lot a frenzy of shouting and shoving. People darted in and out, arms loaded with canned goods and bottled water. Across the street, a brawl spilled onto the sidewalk, fists flying over a pile of looted goods.

Kelsey's pulse quickened. The madness of scarcity had hit this town hard—either it had just begun, or it hadn't stopped since the EMP.

"We need to move," she whispered, steering Anna toward a quieter parking lot nearby. They skirted the crowd, keeping their heads down as screams and the crash of breaking glass echoed behind them. Kelsey glanced back, her stomach churning as she saw flames licking up bushes near the store, windows shattering under thrown bricks.

"Why are they going so crazy?" Anna asked, her voice barely audible over the noise and chaos behind them.

"Food," Kelsey said grimly. "No power, no trucks, no deliveries. Supply's low, demand's high. People are desperate.”

Anna's eyes widened. “I hope there's something left when I get back to Georgia.”

Kelsey's thoughts turned to her son, Parker, back in Tennessee. “If Parker remembers what I taught him, he'll have hit the stores early. He's smart—he'll be fine.”

“You really think he's okay on his own?” Anna asked, her tone soft but probing.

Kelsey's chest tightened, but she kept her voice steady. “Yes. He's eighteen, and I've drilled survival into him since he was a kid. He'll manage.” She paused, then added, “I just wish I'd been home when this hit. I hate not being there for him.”

Anna reached out, squeezing her arm. “I'm sorry. I didn't mean to—”

“It's fine.” Kelsey cut her off, softening. “I'm just... frustrated. Let's keep moving.”

They pressed on, the town's chaos fading behind them as they reached the eastern outskirts. After an hour of brisk walking, their legs heavy from the rush, Kelsey called for a break. They sank onto a grassy patch beside the highway, the distant sound of gunfire now just a memory. Anna rubbed her forehead, wincing, but her steps had been steadier than Kelsey expected. Maybe she was tougher than she looked.

~

Parker Davidson

Parker flipped the last pancake onto a plate, the sizzle of eggs filling the kitchen with a comforting aroma.

He was using up the last of the perishable food—eggs, sausage, anything that wouldn't last without refrigeration. Over the next few days, he planned to cook everything in the fridge and freezer to avoid waste. The EMP had changed everything, and every bite mattered.

He stepped into the bedroom, gently shaking Sydney awake. She groaned but followed him to the dining room, her eyes lighting up at the sight of pancakes, eggs, and a steaming mug of coffee.

"When'd you get up?" she asked, digging in.

"About an hour after sunrise," Parker said, sliding into a chair across from her. "Wanted to get a head start on cooking the perishables. They won't last much longer."

Sydney nodded, savoring a bite. "When do you want to head to the meeting?"

"Soon as we're done eating," he replied. "Don't want to miss anything."

"Sounds good," Sydney said, finishing her plate. "I'll get dressed and be ready."

They cleaned up quickly, the clatter of dishes a brief return to normalcy. Parker grabbed his pistol from the counter, tucked it into his holster, and they headed out, the morning air cool against their skin.

The grocery store parking lot was a short walk, and they arrived just as a crowd gathered around an old city bus, its roof converted into an impromptu stage. A staircase led to a podium where the mayor stood, scanning the growing crowd.

Parker and Sydney edged closer, blending into the crowd. The mayor cleared his throat, his voice carrying over the murmurs.

"Welcome, citizens of Oak Hill. As you know, an EMP has hit the country, disrupting everything. My job—my hope—is to keep this town from descending into chaos. We'll keep the police on duty, stores open, and work toward rebuilding. Questions?" He was tired of saying the same things day after day.

A man near the front raised his hand. "What about currency? Are we switching to bartering?"

The mayor adjusted his glasses. "I'd prefer to keep cash in use, but bartering's likely to take hold. If you run a business, it's your call—cash or trade. Next?"

Another man, closer to Parker, spoke up, "Is this EMP the start of an attack? An invasion?"

The mayor hesitated, his expression tightening. "It's possible, but I'm focused on getting us through this, not speculating on causes."

Murmurs rippled through the crowd, and a voice shouted, "What's your plan if it is an attack?"

The mayor stepped back, his face unreadable. "I'm not addressing that now."

He turned, descending the bus stairs, flanked by riot police who escorted him toward city hall across the lot.

Parker glanced at Sydney, raising an eyebrow. "That was... short."

"Yeah," she said, frowning. "Let's get home and get our stuff done."

They joined the dispersing crowd, weaving through the parking lot as neighbors peeled off toward their homes. Back on their street, Parker's steps slowed as he spotted a man in their driveway, a shotgun slung over his shoulder. The stranger's boots and jeans were caked with mud, a burnt-out cigarette dangling from his lips. His scruffy beard and buzzcut gave him a rough edge, and Parker's hand hovered near his pistol.

The man's eyes locked on Sydney. "Sydney!" he bellowed.

Sydney froze, her face paling. "Uh-oh," she muttered.

"Who is he?" Parker asked, keeping his voice low.

"My dad," she said, her tone bitter. "Haven't seen him in years. After what he did to my mom, I hoped I never would."

Parker nodded, his jaw tight. "Let's stay calm."

As they approached, the man's voice grew sharper. "I went to Mary's house. You weren't there, so I figured you were shacked up with him." He jerked his head toward Parker.

"Why are you here?" Sydney asked, crossing her arms.

"You're coming with me. I'll keep you safe until the power's back."

"No," Sydney said flatly. "I'm staying here."

"You're not staying with this kid," her father snapped, his hand tightening on the shotgun's sling. "Pack your things. Now."

Parker stepped forward, his voice steady. "She said she's not going. You need to leave."

The man's eyes narrowed, and he tossed the cigarette to the ground.

"Who the hell do you think you're talking to?" He

swung the shotgun up, aiming it at Parker. "You've got three seconds to come with me, Sydney, or I shoot him."

Parker's heart raced, but before he could react, Sydney's hand moved in a blur, snatching the pistol from his holster. The shot rang out, deafening, and Parker's ears screamed as the man crumpled to the grass, the shotgun clattering beside him. Sydney stood frozen, the pistol trembling in her hands, her face a mask of shock.

Parker gently took the gun, his pulse pounding. "You okay?"

She didn't answer, her eyes locked on her father's body.

"Parker?" a voice called. Preston, their neighbor, jogged over, his face etched with concern. "What happened?"

Parker pulled him aside, keeping his voice low. "Her dad showed up, tried to force her to go with him. Things went south."

Preston glanced at the body, then back at Parker. "Need help?"

"Yeah," Parker said. "Can you help me bury him? I want this done quietly."

Preston nodded. They grabbed shovels from the garage and set to work in the backyard, digging a shallow grave under the fading daylight. As they worked, they traded stories of the past few days, the chaos in town, the uncertainty of the future. When the task was done, Preston clapped Parker on the shoulder and headed home to his family.

Parker returned the shovels to the garage and found Sydney inside, curled on the couch with Nala nestled against her.

"You doing okay?" he asked, his voice soft.

"I guess," she said, her voice hollow. "I never thought I'd have to... do that."

"I know." Parker sat beside her, searching for words but finding none. "I'm gonna make some food. Want a plate?"

She nodded faintly, stroking Nala's fur.

In the kitchen, Parker pulled out a few pounds of ground beef from the freezer, thawing it on the counter. He'd cook it all over the next few days, starting with a pound tonight. As he broke up the meat in a skillet, sprinkling taco seasoning over it, his mind wandered.

The mayor's talk of cash had him thinking—could he get to the bank tomorrow, withdraw what they had? Money might still hold value, at least for now, and they'd need every advantage to face whatever came next.

Chapter 7

Parker Davidson

The morning sun barely crested the horizon as Parker and Sydney stepped out of the house, their boots scuffing the quiet street. Sydney was still shaken from the confrontation with her father the day before, her eyes distant, but she'd agreed to join Parker on a trip to the bank. They needed cash—something tangible in a world where power and certainty had vanished. Leaving early was deliberate; the fewer people who saw them carrying bags of money, the better.

The bank stood eerily silent, its glass doors reflecting the pale dawn. Inside, only a pair of tellers and two police officers lingered, the latter stationed near the entrance, their hands resting on holstered sidearms to keep the peace. Sydney sank into a cushioned chair in the lobby, her gaze fixed on the floor, while Parker approached the counter.

"How can I help you today?" the teller asked, her voice professional but strained, as if the past few days had worn her thin.

"I need to withdraw some cash from my account,"

Parker said, sliding his ID across the counter.

"Do you have your account number?" she asked, her fingers hovering over a notepad.

Parker recited the number, answering her follow-up questions about his address and mother's maiden name. The teller rose, disappearing into a back room, her flashlight beam cutting through the dimness as she rifled through a file cabinet. She returned with a stapled stack of papers, flipping through them to find his latest statement. "Here's your account info," she said, handing him the papers.

Parker scanned the numbers. "Looks right," he confirmed, his voice steady despite the weight of the moment.

"How much do you want to withdraw?" the teller asked, her pen poised.

He glanced at the balance again, calculating. "Ten thousand." Enough to cover necessities without drawing too much attention—or so he hoped.

The teller's eyes widened, a flicker of disbelief crossing her face. She gave him a look that screamed, "Are you serious?" but Parker just nodded.

Without a word, she stood again, crossing the room to whisper with another teller. Their hushed voices were indecipherable, but the urgency was clear. After a moment, she returned.

"Can you come with me to the back, please?"

Parker hesitated, his instincts prickling, but he nodded. "Sure."

She led him through a half-door to a small, windowless meeting room, its walls lined with faded motivational posters.

"Wait here," she said, leaving him alone.

Parker sat, the chair creaking under him, and tried to ignore the unease creeping up his spine. Ten minutes later, the teller returned, dropping two heavy duffle bags onto the table with a thud.

"Here's your ten thousand dollars."

"Thanks," Parker said, standing and grabbing the bags. The weight surprised him—far heavier than he'd expected. Coins, he realized, mixed with bills to make up the amount.

The teller cleared her throat. "Since you're taking that much, would you like a police escort to ensure you get home safely?"

Parker thought for a moment, weighing the risk of drawing attention against the security of extra protection. "Yeah. Please. Better safe than sorry."

She nodded. "Let's head back out front."

In the lobby, Sydney stood as Parker emerged, the duffle bags slung over his shoulders.

"Ready?" she asked, her voice quiet but steady.

"They're sending an officer with us," Parker said, nodding toward the two policemen approaching.

"Sergeant Harrison," the taller officer said, extending a hand. "This is Sergeant Landon." His grip was firm, his eyes scanning Parker and Sydney with practiced caution.

"Parker," he replied, shaking Harrison's hand. "This is Sydney."

"Good to meet you," Harrison said, his tone

professional but warm. "How far are we going?"

"Just down the road," Parker said. "Half a mile, maybe less."

The officers nodded, and the group stepped into the morning light. The duffle bags dug into Parker's shoulders, their weight a constant reminder of the coins rattling inside. He'd known money was heavy, but this was brutal—fifty pounds per bag, he guessed. Gritting his teeth, he pushed through the ache, determined to get home before trouble found them.

At the neighborhood's entrance, marked by a weathered wooden sign, Sergeant Landon glanced at Parker. "Your turn to lead, kid."

Parker managed a grin. "Guess I have to."

He took point, though the bags slowed his pace to a plod. Fifteen minutes later, they turned onto their street, the familiar sight of their house easing the tension in his chest.

The officers stopped at the sidewalk, watching Parker and Sydney reach the porch. With a nod, they turned back toward the bank, their duty done.

"Holy hell, these are heavy," Parker groaned, dropping the bags onto the porch with a metallic clunk.

Sydney raised an eyebrow. "Sounds like you got more than just bills in there."

"Yeah, coins, too," Parker said, dragging the bags inside to the dining room. He hoisted them onto the table and unzipped them, revealing stacks of bills and rolls of quarters, dimes, and nickels. Methodically, he sorted the money, counting each stack to confirm the total: ten thousand dollars, exactly as promised. Satisfied, he repacked the bags and zipped them shut, leaving them on the table for now.

"I'm gonna start on the basement," he said, wiping his hands on his jeans. Their plan for the day was to organize their supplies—food, water, tools—to make everything accessible in the chaos of the post-EMP world. A tidy house meant a clearer mind, and they'd need both to survive.

Sydney nodded, heading to the garage. "I'll tackle the stuff out there."

Parker started toward the basement but paused, realizing the pitch-black space would be impossible to navigate without light. He doubled back to the garage, nearly colliding with Sydney.

"Thought you were cleaning the basement?" she asked, brushing a strand of hair from her face.

"I am," Parker said, stepping to the workbench. "Just need a headlamp."

Sydney gestured to the cluttered tools around them. "What should we do with all this?"

Parker rifled through a drawer, pulling out a headlamp. He clicked it on—nothing. "Battery," he muttered, swapping it for a fresh one. The light flickered to life. "Let's move the workbench and toolbox closer to the door. We can store hardware there and shift the basement stuff to the spare room upstairs—the one Mom wanted to turn into a gym. It's less cluttered, and the house is safer than the garage if someone tries to break in."

Sydney nodded. "Smart. I'll get started."

Parker returned to the basement, able to see much

more with the headlamp. The basement had a bedroom, a living room, and a utility room, all becoming a catch-all for excess belongings. Most of the shelves were things from Parker's childhood as well as keepsakes and memorabilia from his grandparents.

He started on one wall, pulling down boxes of Christmas decorations—ornaments, tinsel, lights that no longer worked. He hauled them upstairs to the dining room, setting them aside for now. The next box held butane canisters for their camp stove, which he left on the shelf. Box by box, he sorted through the clutter, carrying away what could be moved to the spare room upstairs. By the time the dining room was nearly full, Sydney joined him, grabbing a box of old photo albums.

"Garage is mostly done," she said, hefting the box. "Food and water are ready to go downstairs."

"Great," Parker said, picking up another box. "Let's get these upstairs first."

The spare room, a modest space the size of Parker's bedroom, filled quickly with boxes. On their fourth trip, a knock at the front door interrupted them. Parker set his box down and answered it, finding Preston on the porch, holding a walkie-talkie.

"Hey, Parker," Preston said, handing him the radio. "Thought this might help with communication."

Parker turned the device over, noting a sticky note with "*Channel 32*" scrawled on it.

"This works?" he asked, pressing the power button. Static crackled to life.

"Yeah," Preston said. "Me and my wife got into prepping a while back. Built Faraday cages for some electronics—radios, flashlights, stuff like that."

"That's genius," Parker said, genuinely impressed. "Didn't know you could protect stuff from an EMP."

"Took some research, but it's simple enough," Preston said. "Got anyone else who might need one? I have three more, not counting ours."

Parker thought for a moment. "Leo, three houses down. He's been helping out—could use one."

"I'll swing by his place," Preston said. "Channel 32's our frequency. Call if you need anything."

"Thanks, man," Parker said, clipping the radio to his belt. "This'll be a game-changer."

"Be safe," Preston called, stepping off the porch.

Parker returned to the dining room where Sydney pointed to the radio on his belt. "What's that?"

"Preston's," Parker explained. "He protected it in a Faraday cage. Works like a charm. He's giving one to Leo, too."

"That's huge for staying in touch," Sydney said, setting down a box. "Let's finish these and move the food downstairs. Should fill up those shelves."

They hauled cases of water and canned goods to the basement, organizing them by type—beans, soups, vegetables. When they finished, the shelves were packed, a reassuring stockpile against an uncertain future. Parker grabbed the duffle bags of money and stashed them next to the shelves, out of sight.

Upstairs, Sydney collapsed onto the couch, Nala curling up beside her for a nap. Parker grabbed a water bottle from the kitchen, chugging it and crushing the plastic before capping it. He slipped into his room, pulling a handful of bills and coin rolls from one of the duffle bags and tucking them into his backpack. Cash might still hold weight—for now.

Outside, he surveyed the backyard, envisioning a chicken coop. Fresh eggs would be a godsend. He measured the space with a tape measure—tight, but enough for a small coop. In the garage, he found a pile of lumber, enough to start the project. He set up sawhorses, marked the wood, and began cutting, the handsaw's slow rhythm testing his patience.

A beep from the radio on the patio table interrupted him. He grabbed it, switching to channel 32. Static hissed, followed by Leo's voice. "Test. Test. Test."

Parker chuckled, keying the mic. "We hear you, Leo. What's up?"

"Just checking if it works," Leo said, his grin audible through the static.

"It does," Parker replied. "Preston, you there?"

"What's up, kid?" Preston's voice crackled through.

"You still got those chickens?" Parker asked. "I'm building a coop—thought I could take a few off your hands."

"Got a dozen," Preston said. "You need help with the coop?"

"I need supplies," Parker admitted. "Wood, nails, chicken feed. My truck's dead, though. And a mile down the road."

"Mine's running," Preston said. "Swing by now, and we'll go hit the hardware store."

"Hell, yeah," Parker said. "Give me a sec to grab my stuff."

He clipped the radio to his jeans, grabbed his backpack and pistol, and headed out, careful not to wake Sydney. Across the street, Preston's rebuilt Dodge Ram idled, its sleek black finish gleaming despite the dust. Parker climbed in, the engine roaring as they pulled out.

"What do you need at the store?" Preston asked, navigating the empty streets.

"Wood—2x4s, 4x4s, plywood. Nails, screws, chicken feed. Enough to tackle any project," Parker said.

Preston nodded. "I'll grab some stuff for myself, too. You'll need straw for the coop floor—tear it up, spread it out. Keeps the chickens comfortable."

"Got it," Parker said, mentally adding it to his list.

The hardware store parking lot was a graveyard of stalled cars. They grabbed carts, loading them with lumber, feed, and straw bales until they overflowed. At the checkout, a grizzled cashier raised an eyebrow. "Building a house?"

"Maybe," Parker quipped.

"Since you're getting a haul, how's five hundred sound?" the cashier offered, clearly too tired to haggle.

Parker glanced at Preston, who nodded.

"Deal." He pulled five hundred-dollar bills from his backpack, handing them over.

"Be safe," the cashier called as they left.

The truck bed sagged under the weight, the plywood barely fitting. They drove slowly, the load shifting with every turn.

Parker keyed the radio. "Leo, meet us at my place. Need your help unloading."

"Ugh, with what?" Leo teased. "Kidding. I'm on my way."

"He's a comedian, huh?" Preston said, chuckling.

"Wants to be," Parker replied. "Not holding my breath."

They pulled into the driveway, the truck groaning to a stop. Leo jogged over, eyeing the load. "Jesus, you buy the whole store?"

"Better to have it than need it," Parker said, opening the garage door. They unloaded the wood, stacking it neatly beside his mom's dead car. Space ran tight, so Parker grabbed the keys, shifted the car into neutral, and, with Preston and Leo's help, pushed it across the street to the curb.

Sydney appeared in the garage doorway, rubbing sleep from her eyes. "What's all this noise?" She froze, spotting the pile. "When did you get all this?"

"Fifteen minutes ago," Parker said, glancing at Preston and Leo for confirmation. "Building a chicken coop for fresh eggs."

Sydney raised an eyebrow. "Rather have it than need it, right?"

"Exactly," Parker said, grinning.

They finished unloading, sorting nails and screws into the toolbox. Leo dropped a 2x4, wincing.

"This is a lot," he said. "You sure about this?"

"Chickens are simple," Preston said, setting a straw bale outside. "You'll be fine."

Parker turned to Preston. "So, who else is getting a radio?"

"My buddy Chris, across town," Preston said. "He runs a clinic. Good to have a doctor on our channel. Got two more radios if you know anyone."

Parker shook his head. "Most of my friends aren't ready for this. You, Leo?"

"Nah," Leo said. "But I'll let you know."

They wrapped up, shutting the garage and settling on the porch to talk. The conversation drifted from supplies to strategies, the weight of the new world pressing in. As dusk fell, they parted ways, promising to check in on channel 32. Parker headed inside, the radio's static a faint reminder of the fragile connections holding their world together.

Chapter 8
Kelsey Davidson

Idaho Falls, Idaho

Kelsey and Anna stepped out of the dusty sedan, the engine still ticking as it cooled in the morning heat. The man who'd given them a ride—a grizzled traveler heading southeast—had dropped them off in Idaho Falls, nearly four hundred miles closer to home. It was a generous offer, but it left them in the last place they wanted to be: another town, its quiet streets hiding potential threats. The sign they'd passed on the way in pegged the population at under two hundred, but after their chaotic trek through other towns, Kelsey wasn't taking chances.

"Let's move fast," she said, adjusting her backpack. "In and out, then we keep pushing east and south."

Anna nodded, her face pale under the bandage on her forehead. "Can we grab some food if we find any? We're running low."

"Sure," Kelsey replied, her hand brushing the pistol at her hip for reassurance. "But we stay sharp."

They walked past the first weathered building, a shuttered gas station with cracked windows. The town was quieter than expected—only a handful of people stirred, tending small gardens or hauling water from a well. The stillness felt unnatural, like the calm before a storm. As they ventured deeper, the silence was broken only by the crunch of gravel under their boots and the occasional creak of a porch swing.

They spotted a small grocery store, its sign faded but intact. Kelsey peered through the grimy windows, scanning for movement. "Looks clear," she said, pushing the door open. The hinges groaned, and the dim interior smelled of dust and stale air. Most shelves were bare, picked clean by looters or desperate locals, but a few snack items—crackers, jerky, a lone bag of dried fruit—remained. They grabbed what they could, stuffing their packs carefully. In another aisle, they found a handful of canned goods—beans, peaches, and a dented can of spaghetti. Kelsey hesitated, weighing the added weight against their need.

"Let's keep it light," she said. "We'll hit another town soon."

Anna nodded, slipping a can of peaches into her bag. "This'll do for now."

They slipped out of the store, moving quickly through the town's southeastern edge. In the distance, a plume of black smoke curled into the sky, stark against the clear blue. As they neared the highway, the source became clear: a plane wreck smoldered in a field, its twisted fuselage half-buried in scorched earth. The fire had spread, charring acres of grass and leaving a haze that stung their eyes. Kelsey's stomach turned—any survivors would've been engulfed.

They hurried along the highway, the smoke thickening as they passed the heart of the blaze. A herd of cows, spooked by the crash, had broken through a fence into a neighboring field, their mooing faint over the crackle of flames. Once upwind, the air cleared, and Kelsey's lungs welcomed the relief.

They pushed on, unwilling to stop until they were well clear of the wreckage. Finding no cover, they settled behind a pair of abandoned cars on the roadside, their rusted frames offering minimal protection.

Kelsey dropped her pack and pulled out two cans of spaghetti, handing one to Anna along with a spoon. "Cold, but it's food," she said, popping the lid. They ate in silence, the metallic tang of the sauce a small comfort after days of granola bars and jerky. Before they moved on, Kelsey checked Anna's bandage. The wound was clean, no signs of infection, but the gauze was fraying. They'd need more supplies soon.

The sun climbed higher, baking the asphalt as they walked for hours, their shadows stretching long across the road. By late afternoon, exhaustion set in, and Kelsey spotted a ditch lined with dense bushes near a sprawling farm.

"This'll do for tonight," she said, leading Anna down the slope. They nestled close to the bushes, setting up a makeshift camp. Anna collapsed against her pack, wincing, while Kelsey scanned the horizon for threats. Sleep came quickly, though the hard ground offered little comfort.

~

The next morning, a shout jolted Kelsey awake.

"Who are you?" a raspy voice demanded.

She blinked against the sun, squinting at a man

looming above, his shotgun trained on her. His weathered face was framed by a graying beard, his eyes sharp but not cruel.

Kelsey raised her hands slowly. "We're just passing through. Needed a place to sleep. Been traveling since the EMP hit."

The man lowered the shotgun slightly, his posture easing. "Where you coming from?"

"Everett, Washington," Kelsey said, sitting up to block the sun's glare. "Heading to Tennessee."

He nodded, his expression softening. "Long haul. You two want some breakfast before you go?"

"Yes, please," Anna piped up, her voice hoarse but eager.

The man gestured toward a farmhouse a quarter-mile down the road. "Name's Neil. Come by when you're ready."

He turned, his boots crunching on the gravel as he headed back.

Anna was already rolling up her jacket which had doubled as a sleeping pad. "What are you waiting for? I'm starving."

Kelsey groaned, her muscles screaming from days of walking. "Hold on. I'm sore as hell. Let's take it slow today."

Anna touched her bandage, wincing. "Yeah. My head's killing me, but I'll manage."

They packed up, shouldered their bags, and trudged down the road to the farmhouse. Pastures flanked the path, dotted with grazing cows and horses, their calm grazing a stark contrast to the chaos of the cities. The house came into view, a sturdy two-story with peeling paint and three battered cars parked out front. Kelsey's pulse quickened—working vehicles could change everything.

Anna knocked on the door, and Neil answered, waving them inside. The kitchen smelled of bacon and eggs, an aroma that made Kelsey's stomach rumble.

A woman with kind eyes and flour-dusted hands stood at the stove, flipping toast. "I'm Ellen," she said, smiling. "Take as much as you want."

Kelsey and Anna sat at the worn oak table, piling their plates with scrambled eggs, crispy bacon, and buttered toast.

"Thank you, Ellen," Kelsey said, savoring the smoky bite of bacon. "This is a godsend."

"Where you headed?" Ellen asked, spreading jam on her toast.

"Nashville, Tennessee," Kelsey replied. "We started in Everett. It's been... a journey."

"That's a trek," Neil said, leaning back in his chair. "You want a shower? We've got a well and solar panels. Water's cold, but it works."

Anna's eyes lit up. "You have a working shower?"

"No batteries to store power, so no showers at night," Neil explained. "But it's yours if you want it."

"That'd be amazing," Kelsey said, finishing her plate. "If it's not too much trouble."

"Go ahead," Ellen said, waving toward the hall. "Towels are in the bathroom."

Neil stood, setting his plate in the sink. Kelsey

followed suit, but Ellen shook her head. "I've got it. You're guests."

"You go first," Anna said to Kelsey, grabbing another strip of bacon. "I need to figure out how to keep this bandage dry."

"I'll help when you're ready," Kelsey offered, grabbing her bag and heading to the bathroom. Neil met her in the hall, pointing to a stack of towels on the counter.

"Water's ice-cold," he warned.

"Good," Kelsey said with a wry smile. "Might calm my nerves."

She stepped into the shower, gasping as the frigid water hit her skin. Using shampoo as soap, she scrubbed her clothes first, rinsing them and hanging them on the shower rod. Then she washed herself, the cold water stripping away days of grime and sweat. Clean for the first time in a week, she felt human again.

She dried off, changed into fresh clothes, and let her hair air-dry, too tired to fuss with it. Kelsey grabbed her now clean clothes and took them outside to hang on a clothesline.

Back in the kitchen, Anna was reading an old newspaper, grease-stained from breakfast.

"Your turn," Kelsey said.

Anna headed to the bathroom, and moments later, a muffled yelp signaled the cold water's shock.

Kelsey chuckled, picking up the newspaper—a local edition, months old, with headlines about crop yields and county fairs.

Anna returned, her hair damp but her bandage

intact, carrying her wet clothes.

"Clothesline's out back," Ellen said, nodding toward the door.

Returning inside, she turned to Neil and Ellen. "Is there anything we can do to repay you? You've been so kind."

Neil waved her off. "You didn't take anything we wouldn't have used ourselves."

Kelsey hesitated, then took a chance. "I know it's a big ask, but... Any chance we could borrow one of those cars out front?"

Neil exchanged a glance with Ellen, who gave a slight nod. "Sure," he said, pulling a set of keys from his pocket and handing them to Kelsey. "It's yours."

Kelsey's jaw dropped, gratitude overwhelming her. "Thank you. I can't say it enough."

"Be safe," Neil said, his voice gruff but sincere. "There's three out there. At my age, I'm not doing much with them, especially in times like these."

The pair went out to the back porch and grabbed their clothes from the clothes line, neatly folding them. Back inside they slipped on their shoes, shouldered their packs, and stepped outside.

The vehicle—a beat-up old truck—smelled of mildew and baked vinyl, but it started with a cough when Kelsey turned the key. She buckled her seatbelt, Anna did the same, and they pulled out of the driveway, the dirt road crunching under the tires.

As they merged onto the highway, Kelsey glanced at Anna, whose face was still pale but determined. With a working car, Tennessee felt a little closer.

~

Parker Davidson

Parker stumbled into the kitchen, his body heavy with exhaustion despite the new day. He filled a glass with water, sipping slowly as he let Nala out the back door to romp in the yard. Sitting at the dining room table, he mentally mapped out his tasks: finish the chicken coop, water the garden, stay vigilant. The world was unraveling and every step mattered.

He refilled his glass, let Nala back in, and headed to his room to dress. Digging through the closet, he found an old cowboy hat, its brim faded but sturdy. It'd keep the sun out of his eyes—a small win. Dressed and ready, he stepped outside, Nala trailing behind, and eyed the corner of the backyard where his chicken coop would stand. The sawhorses from yesterday's woodcutting waited nearby.

In the garage, he opened both doors, letting in the morning light, and rummaged through the toolbox for nails and a hammer. Back in the yard, he laid out the lumber, nailing boards into a sturdy frame for the coop's base. He topped it with plywood, nailing it down, but an overhang jutted out awkwardly. Grabbing the handsaw, he trimmed it flush, tossing the scraps into a growing pile. Layer by layer, he built the walls, the structure rising to his height. The roof came next—a plywood sheet nailed securely, with excess cut away and added to the sides for stability.

Sweating, he dragged the coop to the yard's corner, ensuring it was snug against the fence. He had returned his tools to the garage, organizing them neatly, when footsteps crunched behind him. Preston stood there, hands in his pockets.

"Morning," Parker said, wiping his brow. "You're up early."

"Saw you working when I got up," Preston said. "Couldn't sleep?"

"Nope," Parker admitted. "Mind helping me spread straw in the coop?"

"Grab a bale, and I'll show you how," Preston said.

Parker hauled a straw bale to the backyard, dropping it in front of the coop. Preston tore off handfuls, scattering them across the floor until a quarter of the bale was gone, creating a soft bedding. Parker peeked inside, memorizing the amount for next time, then dragged the bale back to the garage.

"Got a box for the chickens?" Preston asked.

"Yeah," Parker said, pulling a large cardboard box from a shelf. They crossed the street to Preston's house, where his wife, Angelina, and three-year-old daughter, Bella, greeted them warmly. Parker smiled—Bella's growth over the years was a bright spot in his memories. They headed to Preston's coop, selecting four healthy chickens and securing them in the box.

Back at Parker's, they released the chickens into the coop. Three scurried inside, pecking at the walls, while the fourth lingered outside. Parker grabbed a handful of feed from the garage, sprinkling it near the coop's entrance to lure them in.

"Thanks for these."

"Get those eggs going early. I gotta run—Angelina's making breakfast."

"Catch you later," Parker called as Preston walked down the driveway.

Inside, Parker nearly tripped over Nala, who'd been waiting at the back door. He let her in and started breakfast, using the last of their eggs and mixing pancake batter from the pantry. As the pancakes sizzled, Sydney shuffled into the kitchen, rubbing her eyes.

"Breakfast's almost ready," Parker said, flipping the eggs. "Coop's done, and the chickens are in."

"Nice," Sydney said, slumping at the table. "When'd you get up?"

"Dunno," Parker said, plating the food. He split the eggs and gave each of them two pancakes, saving the rest for later. They ate quickly, the warm food a brief comfort. After cleaning the dishes, they sank onto the living room couch, Nala sprawling between them.

"I'm gonna water the plants," Parker said, standing.

In the garage, he grabbed a five-gallon bucket of water but realized pouring it directly would drown the garden. He rummaged through shelves, finding his mom's watering can, and carefully filled it. Outside, he tended the garden beds, the soil darkening as he watered the seeds. Neighbors milled about, but the street was quiet—until gunshots cracked in the distance.

Parker bolted inside, grabbing the radio from the kitchen. He beeped Leo and Preston.

"You hear that?" he asked as they picked up.

"Gunshots," Preston confirmed. "Sounded like they were shooting at our neighbors."

"We should check it out," Parker said.

"Meet you outside," Leo replied, the radio clicking

off.

Parker grabbed his pistol, holstering it at his waist. Sydney stood, alarmed. "What's going on?"

"Gunshots," Parker said, "Me, Leo, and Preston are going to investigate."

"Be safe," she said, kissing him quickly.

"I will." He promised, sprinting out the door.

Preston and Leo were already waiting, armed and tense. "Which house?" Parker asked.

"Three or four that way," Leo said, pointing down the street.

They ran toward where they heard the shots, being led into the backyard of a house a block down from theirs. In the backyard, they found two men holding a family of four at gunpoint. Preston and Leo moved swiftly, dragging the men to the gate while Parker took their guns.

Preston held his pistol on the men, his voice sharp. "Why the hell are you doing this?"

"We needed food," one stammered, tears in his eyes. "Please, don't shoot."

"There are better ways to get food," Preston snapped.

The other man scoffed. "You think cash still matters? I ditched mine day one."

"Your mistake," Preston said. "Leave. Now. And don't come back."

The men hesitated, reaching for their guns, but Leo kicked them away. "Not happening."

"Those are our only protection," one protested.

"Should've thought of that before you pulled this stunt," Preston said. "Go."

The men stumbled off, muttering about the chaos coming too soon.

Parker shook his head. "This shouldn't be happening yet."

"Agreed," Preston said. "Let's check on the family."

In the backyard, the family sat at a patio table, shaken but unharmed.

"You okay?" Parker asked.

The woman nodded, her voice trembling. "It was terrifying, but we're fine."

"We're down the street," Preston said. "Holler if you need us."

"Thank you," she whispered.

They returned to the street, ready to head home. "We need to get Chris, my doctor friend, from across town. Things are worse over there—homeless camps, looters. He'd be safer with us."

"When do we go?" Parker asked.

"Soon as possible," Preston said. "Tomorrow at the latest."

"Let's go now. I'll get Sydney," Parker said. "We'll be ready. I'll radio you."

Preston nodded, jogging home. Parker entered the house, calling upstairs. "Sydney?"

"Up here," she replied. "Just poking through the stuff we moved yesterday. Got bored."

"We're going across town with Preston," Parker said.

"His friend Chris, a doctor, needs to relocate here. Another set of eyes would help."

"Why's he moving?" Sydney asked, descending the stairs.

"It's rougher on his side of town," Parker said. "A doctor's a good asset."

Sydney grabbed her pistol, holstering it. "I'm ready."

Parker checked his backpack, ensuring he had cash, ammo, and the radio. With Sydney by his side, he stepped outside, the weight of the rifle on his shoulder a reminder of the dangers waiting beyond their quiet street.

Chapter 9

Kelsey Davidson

Pinedale, Wyoming

The old Chevy rattled into Pinedale, Wyoming, its engine coughing like a smoker. Kelsey glanced at Anna, slumped against the passenger window, her soft snores barely audible over the hum of the tires. The bandage on Anna's forehead, stained with a faint rust of dried blood, caught the morning light filtering through the cracked windshield.

Kelsey's eyes swept the town's main street, a narrow strip of cracked asphalt lined with faded storefronts. People milled about—trading jars of preserves, hauling bundles of firewood, their voices a low, steady hum of purpose. The calm of it struck her like a cold splash of water. After the chaos of looted highways and gunfire in Oregon, Pinedale felt like a pocket of forgotten normalcy.

She eased the truck to a stop outside a general store, its sign reading "Pinedale Provisions" in chipped red paint. If they could score gas here, they might cut days off the trek to Nashville. Kelsey killed the engine, the sudden silence amplifying the distant clatter of a cart rolling by.

"Stay put," she murmured to Anna, who stirred but

didn't wake. Stepping out, her boots crunched on gravel, and a faint breeze carried the scent of pine and dust. A gas-powered generator growled outside the store, its vibrations pulsing through the ground.

Inside, the air was thick with the musty tang of old wood and leather. Shelves stood half-empty, stocked with mismatched cans and tools, a testament to the town's stubborn resilience. A man behind the counter—grizzled with a salt-and-pepper beard and eyes like chipped flint—looked up from a ledger.

"Need any help, ma'am?"

"Any chance you're pumping gas?" Kelsey asked, keeping her tone even, though her fingers twitched near the knife at her belt.

He leaned back, sizing her up. "Where you headed?"

"Tennessee," she said. "Saw your generator out front. Figured it might mean working pumps."

The man chuckled, a dry sound like rustling leaves. "Tennessee's a haul. Lucky you've got a rig old enough to dodge whatever fried the grid." He stood, brushing his hands on his flannel shirt. "I'll fill your tank and a spare can. Might get you a ways toward home."

Kelsey's shoulders loosened, but suspicion lingered like a habit. "That's generous. What's the catch?"

"Ain't one," he said, meeting her gaze. "Been giving gas to anyone with a working vehicle. Figure it's my way of keeping folks moving. Gas don't do me no good sitting in the ground."

She nodded, gratitude tempered by caution. "Means more than you know. How can I repay you?"

He waved her off, heading for the door. "Just get

where you're going. World's messy enough."

Outside, he flipped a switch on the generator, and it roared louder, spitting a faint whiff of exhaust. He grabbed a dented red gas can from beside the pump, filling it with a steady stream of fuel. Handing it to her, he said, "Fill your tank. I'll top this off after."

Kelsey poured the gas, the sharp scent stinging her nose as it glugged into the car's tank. The man watched, arms crossed, his weathered face unreadable. When she handed the can back, he refilled it with practiced ease, the pump's rhythmic click a rare sound of order.

"Safe travels," he said, tipping his cap as he headed back inside.

She put the can in the bed beside their backpacks before slamming it shut. As she climbed back in, her mind wandered to Parker. Her chest tightened, but she pushed the worry down. He's got the safe, the guns, Sydney. He's tougher than he looks.

Back in the driver's seat, she glanced at Anna, now blinking awake, her eyes bleary but alert.

"We're moving," Kelsey said, turning the key. The engine sputtered to life. "Got gas. Let's eat quick before we go."

Anna's face lit up, hunger cutting through her grogginess. "Food? You're speaking my language."

Kelsey pulled onto a quiet stretch of highway just outside Pinedale, parking beneath a lone cottonwood tree, its leaves rustling in the breeze. She reached into her backpack, pulling out two granola bars and a can of peaches scavenged from the abandoned shuttle van in Oregon. With her pocketknife, she pried open the can, splitting the sweet, syrupy fruit between them, using the lid as Anna's bowl. They ate in silence, the crunch of granola and the faint tang of peaches a fleeting comfort. Anna licked her fingers clean, wincing as her bandage shifted.

"Head still hurt?" Kelsey asked.

"Like a hammer's tapping it," Anna admitted, forcing a grin. "But I'm good. Thanks for playing doctor."

"Don't get used to it," Kelsey said, her tone softening. Anna's resilience was growing on her, a quiet strength beneath the city-girl exterior. Still, the first aid kit was nearly spent—another worry for the road.

They drove for hours, Wyoming's rolling hills flattening into Nebraska's endless plains, the horizon a hazy blur of gold and green. The gas held out longer than Kelsey expected, but as dusk painted the sky in streaks of orange, the engine began moaning, mentioning it was out of fuel. She pulled off near a weathered sign for Sutherland, a speck of a town with a single gas station and a scattering of houses.

"Out of fuel," she said, parking on the roadside. "We camp here tonight."

Anna stretched, her joints popping. "Back to walking tomorrow?"

"Unless luck stays on our side," Kelsey said, grabbing their packs. They set up camp in a cluster of scrubby trees, the air cool and heavy with the scent of dry grass. As they unrolled their sleeping bags—found in the trunk of the car—, a rhythmic clatter broke the silence—a man hammering a fence post into the ground along the road, his flannel shirt stained with sweat. The fence looked like it was hit by a car, the chicken wire wrinkled a couple yards away, with a couple of broken posts beside it.

"Howdy!" he called, leaning on a post, his face creased with age and sun. "Where you folks headed?"

"Tennessee," Kelsey replied, keeping her distance but softening her tone. "Got a working car around?"

The man wiped his brow, squinting. "Got a '76 Chevy pickup in the barn. Runs, barely—alternator's finicky, but the EMP didn't touch it. I don't drive it. No need, staying put."

Kelsey glanced at Anna, who raised an eyebrow, a spark of hope in her eyes. "Third vehicle this week," Anna whispered. "We're charmed."

"Don't jinx it," Kelsey muttered, then turned to the man. "Mind if we take it? We can trade labor—finish that fence, whatever else you need."

He considered, scratching his chin. "Fair deal. Fix the rest of this fence and feed my chickens—collect the eggs, too. Back's too stiff for bending these days. Do that, and the truck's yours, with four five-gallon cans of gas in the bed."

Kelsey's pulse quickened. Another working vehicle could mean reaching Parker in days, not weeks.

"Done," she said, shaking his calloused hand. "I've fixed fences before." He handed her a hammer and a coil of wire, pointing to a toolshed. "Bring the tools to the house when you're done. I'll show you the coop."

Kelsey and Anna set to work, hammering posts and twisting wire as the sun dipped below the horizon. Anna fumbled the wire at first, her fingers clumsy, but Kelsey guided her, showing her how to loop it tight.

"Pull hard," Kelsey said, nodding as Anna got the hang of it. "Not bad for a city girl."

Anna grinned, sweat beading on her forehead. "Learning fast, huh?"

They finished the fence in under an hour, the posts standing sturdy against the darkening sky. Hauling the tools to the man's farmhouse—a sagging, weather-beaten structure with a creaking porch—they knocked on the door.

A gruff "Come in!" echoed from inside. They stepped into a cluttered living room, setting the wire and hammer by the door, the air thick with the smell of woodsmoke and coffee.

"What's next?" Kelsey asked, brushing dirt from her hands.

"Chickens," the man said, leading them to the back door. "Coop's out back. Feed's in a bag on top. Scatter it, grab the eggs."

The coop was a sturdy wooden structure, its paint peeling. Anna opened the feed bag, scattering grain in a wide arc, the chickens clucking and scrambling out. Kelsey slipped inside, collecting a dozen eggs in a wicker basket, their shells warm in her hands. They carried the eggs back to the kitchen, setting them on a worn countertop beside a chipped mug.

The man's eyes crinkled with a smile. "You two don't mess around. Here's your pay." He tossed Kelsey a keyring, the keys glinting in the dim light. "Truck's in the barn. Four gas cans, five gallons each. Should get you a good stretch."

Kelsey caught the keys, her chest swelling with gratitude. She stepped forward, wrapping the man in a quick, fierce hug. "Thank you. This gets me closer to my son."

He patted her shoulder awkwardly. "Get home safe."

They found the truck in the barn, its faded blue paint chipped but the engine coughing to life after a few tries. Kelsey loaded their packs and the gas cans into the bed, her mind racing ahead to Nashville. As they pulled onto the highway, the stars bright overhead, she felt a flicker of hope. Parker was out there, waiting. She'd make it to him, no matter what.

~

Parker Davidson

Parker and Sydney climbed into Preston's Dodge Ram, the worn leather seats creaking as they settled in, the afternoon heat just beginning to kick in, thick with Nashville's summer humidity, carrying the faint tang of smoke from a distant fire.

Sydney sat in the back, her fingers fidgeting with the hem of her faded T-shirt, her eyes shadowed from the weight of yesterday's run-in with her father. Parker caught her gaze in the side mirror, offering a small nod. She returned it, barely, her lips tight. He wanted to say something, but the words stuck—he'd learned to give her space when she got like this.

"How far to Chris's place?" Sydney asked, her voice low, almost lost in the rumble of the engine as Preston pulled out of the driveway.

"Other side of town," Preston said, his hands steady on the wheel, eyes scanning the empty streets. "Ten minutes, maybe twelve if we hit trouble. That neighborhood's rougher than ours, so stay sharp."

Parker nodded, his hand resting on the pistol at his hip, its weight a constant reminder of the world's new rules. He stared out the window as they rolled through Nashville's suburbs, the familiar streets now alien. Trash spilled across lawns—soda cans, torn wrappers, a lone shoe—mingling with the brittle skeletons of dead trees, their branches snapped by looters or storms. The silence was heavy, broken only by the occasional shout or the distant crack of glass. He wondered how long it would take for the city to crumble completely.

They turned into a rundown cul-de-sac, the asphalt cracked and littered with debris. Preston backed the truck into the driveway of a modest house, its windows boarded with warped plywood, a faint smear of graffiti tagging the front door. The air smelled of smoke and something sour, like rotting garbage.

Parker stepped out, his boots crunching on broken glass, and scanned the street. A curtain twitched in a house across the way, but no one emerged. Good. He wasn't in the mood for surprises.

Preston knocked, the sound sharp against the quiet. The door swung open, revealing Chris—a lean man in his forties, his face lined with exhaustion but his eyes sharp, a stethoscope draped around his neck like a lifeline.

"Preston," he said, a tired smile breaking through. "Was about to radio you. Still got my frequency?"

"Slipped my mind," Preston admitted, clapping Chris's shoulder with a grin. "Meant to drop off one of my radios days ago, but things keep piling up. Chris, this is Parker and Sydney, my neighbors."

Chris extended a hand, his grip firm but warm, calluses rough against Parker's palm. "Good to meet you both. Come in—let's make this quick."

The door thudded shut behind them, the deadbolt clicking with a heavy finality. The house was dim, lit by a single camping lantern casting long shadows across cluttered shelves. Medical books lined one wall, their spines cracked from use, while a desk in the corner held stacks of gauze, syringes, and a battered first aid kit. The air smelled faintly of antiseptic and dust.

"We're moving you closer to us," Preston said, his tone matter-of-fact. "Safer in our neighborhood, and we could use a doctor nearby."

Chris ran a hand through his graying hair, sighing. "Figured you'd say that. Alright, let's pack. Sooner we're out, the better."

"Need help?" Parker offered, glancing at Sydney. She nodded, her jaw set, ready to focus on something other than her own thoughts.

"Start in that room," Chris said, pointing down a narrow hallway to a door half-ajar. "Most of my medical supplies are there. Keep it organized—some of it's fragile, and we'll need it ready to use."

Parker and Sydney stepped into the cramped office, its walls lined with metal shelves sagging under the weight of supplies. Bandages, antiseptics, syringes, and vials of medication were neatly arranged, a stark contrast to the chaos outside. Parker grabbed a stack of plastic totes from the corner, handing one to Sydney. "Let's sort this smart," he said. "Bandages in one, meds in another, tools separate. Don't want to dig through a mess if someone's bleeding out."

Sydney nodded, her hands steady as she began packing rolls of gauze.

"You sound like your mom," she said, a faint tease in her voice, though her eyes stayed focused on the task.

Parker snorted, labeling a tote with a marker. "She'd probably say I'm not thorough enough." He mimicked her voice, "'Parker, check the corners, not just the middle!'"

Sydney's laugh, small but genuine, eased the tension in his chest. It was the first time she'd smiled since yesterday.

They worked methodically, sorting supplies with care. Parker tucked vials of antibiotics into a padded bag, remembering his mom's lessons about keeping fragile items secure. Sydney hesitated over a box of syringes, her fingers trembling for a moment before she set them down gently. Parker didn't ask—he knew she'd talk when she was ready.

In the kitchen, Preston was boxing up canned goods—beans, corn, tuna—while Chris stuffed clothes into a duffel bag in the next room. Parker carried a tote to the living room, catching snippets of their conversation. "Got a working car?" he called, setting the tote by the door.

"Yeah, an old Jeep," Chris replied, zipping his bag. "Kept it in a shed with a Faraday cage setup. Learned that from Preston years ago. EMP didn't touch it."

Parker raised an eyebrow, impressed. "Smart. Wish I'd known about Faraday cages before all this."

"Most folks didn't," Chris said, slinging the duffel over his shoulder. "Let's load up."

They hauled the totes and boxes to the truck, Parker jumping into the bed to stack them securely. The medical supplies filled half the space, heavy with the promise of saving lives. Preston handed up boxes of food, while Chris passed a crate of bottled water, his movements quick but careful. Parker tied the load down with rope from Preston's toolbox, sweat beading on his forehead. The street stayed quiet, but he kept one eye on the houses nearby, half-expecting trouble.

"Thanks for the help," Chris said, climbing into the driver's seat of his Jeep, its engine coughing to life.

"We've got you," Preston said, starting the truck.

The convoy rolled out, Preston's Ram leading the way, Chris's Jeep trailing close behind. The streets were quieter than Parker expected, though the distant crash of glass kept his nerves taut. He thought of his mom, wondering where she was—Wyoming, maybe, like Preston had guessed. The thought of her out there, fighting her way to him, made his throat tight. He glanced at Sydney, who was staring out the window, her expression unreadable.

"You okay?" he asked softly.

She nodded, not looking at him. "Just... glad we're helping someone. Feels right."

They reached their neighborhood without incident, backing into Preston's driveway. Chris's Jeep parked behind them, its engine rattling as it shut off.

"Need help unloading?" Parker asked, hopping out of the truck.

"We're good," Chris said, already grabbing a tote. "But I owe you one. Radio me if you need me."

Parker and Sydney crossed the street to their house, Nala greeting them with a joyous wag, her tongue lapping at their hands. The door creaked shut behind them, sealing out the world's chaos for a moment.

"That was easier than I thought it would be," Sydney said, kicking off her sneakers and collapsing onto the couch.

"Yeah," Parker said, holstering his pistol on the counter. "Hope Preston's right about Mom being closer. Wyoming's still a long way off though."

Sydney reached for his hand, her touch warm. "She's tough, Parker. Like you. She'll make it."

He squeezed her hand, grateful for the words, even if doubt gnawed at him. "Let's cook something," he said, needing a distraction. "Mac and cheese?"

Sydney grinned, standing. "Simple and tasty. I'm in."

Parker grabbed two boxes of mac and cheese from the pantry, their bright orange packaging almost blinding.

Sydney poured bottled water into a pot, setting it on the camp stove, the flame hissing softly.

As the water boiled, Parker pulled a Monopoly board from the shelf, its edges worn from years of family game nights. He set it up on the dining table, placing the tiny dog piece for Nala, who watched with a tilted head.

"What's with the game?" Sydney asked, stirring the noodles, the steam curling around her face.

"Figured we could use some fun," Parker said, tossing her the car piece. "You always pick this one."

She caught it, laughing. "You're just mad I always win."

They ate quickly, the cheesy noodles warm and comforting, a brief escape from the weight of the world.

After rinsing their bowls with a splash of water, they dove into the game, their banter filling the room. Sydney's hotels on Boardwalk bankrupted him by the third round, her laughter echoing as he tossed his fake money in defeat. For a few hours, the world outside faded, and it was just them, a board game, and the flicker of a candle.

~

The next morning, a sharp knock jolted Parker awake. He stumbled to the door, rubbing sleep from his eyes, and found Preston waiting on the porch, his daughter Bella bouncing beside him, her pigtails swinging.

"Morning," Preston said, his voice gravelly from lack of sleep. "Going for a walk. You in?"

Parker glanced back at the house, where Sydney was still asleep. "Yeah, give me a sec."

He ducked inside, grabbing his pistol and Nala's leash. In the bedroom, Sydney stirred, her voice muffled. "Who's at the door?"

"Preston," Parker said, clipping the leash on Nala, who wagged furiously. "Wants me to walk with him and Bella. I'll be back."

"Mmm," Sydney murmured, pulling the blanket over her head. "Have fun."

"Ready?" Parker asked, falling into step beside Preston.

"Yep," Preston said, ruffling Bella's hair. "She insisted on coming. Says she's tired of being cooped up."

"Let's go, let's go!" Bella chirped, tugging at Preston's hand.

"Alright, kiddo, we're going," Preston said, kneeling

to her level with a grin. "Don't wear me out."

They walked down the sidewalk, the neighborhood quiet except for the rustle of leaves. Bella skipped ahead, pointing at a bird perched on a sagging power line, while Nala sniffed every mailbox. Parker's thoughts drifted to his mom again, the ache of her absence sharper in the morning light.

"Preston," he said, breaking the silence, "you really think Mom's in Wyoming by now?"

Preston glanced at him, his expression thoughtful. "If she left right away, got a couple of working cars, didn't stop much—she could be. Depends on the roads, the people she meets. But your mom's tough as nails. She's closer than you think."

Parker nodded, clinging to the words. They walked for an hour, looping through the neighborhood, Bella's chatter and Nala's occasional bark filling the silence. By the time they returned, the sun was higher, warming the air.

Parker let Nala into the house, unclipping her leash as she bolted for the kitchen, where Sydney was warming yesterday's pancakes on the camp stove, the sweet scent filling the air.

"Any left?" Parker asked, leaning against the counter.

"Three," Sydney said, sliding a pancake onto her plate. "Pan's still hot if you want them."

"I got it," Parker said, grabbing a plate and tossing the remaining pancakes into the pan. As they sizzled, he watched Sydney, her movements relaxed but her eyes still carrying weight. "You sleep okay?"

"Better than I thought I would," she said, cutting into her pancake. "You?"

"Eh," he said, flipping a pancake. "Kept thinking about Mom."

"She'll get here," Sydney said, her voice firm. "Bet she's bullying her way through some city as we speak."

Parker laughed, the sound easing the knot in his chest. They ate at the dining table, Nala curled at their feet, her tail thumping softly. After washing the plates with a splash of bottled water, Parker sank onto the couch, the quiet of the house settling around him. Then the radio on the counter beeped, a sharp, insistent sound that made him jump.

He grabbed it, switching to Channel 32. "Parker, you there?" Leo's voice crackled through, loud with excitement.

"What's up, Leo?" Parker replied, his heart picking up.

"My mom just got back!" Leo shouted, the words tumbling out. "Walked in an hour ago, like nothing happened!"

Parker's chest tightened, a mix of relief and envy. "That's awesome, man. I'm hoping mine's not far behind."

"Need anything?" Leo asked. "We've got some extra food if you're low."

"We're good for now," Parker said. "Go hang with your mom. Preston and I can handle things."

"Alright, but radio me if anything crazy goes down," Leo said.

"Will do," Parker said, switching off the radio. He set

it down as Sydney walked in, drying her hands on a towel.

"Who was that?" she asked, leaning against the doorway.

"Leo," Parker said, a faint smile tugging at his lips. "His mom made it back."

Sydney's face softened. "That's good news. Means yours and mine aren't far off."

"Yeah," Parker said, meeting her eyes. "Hope so."

Chapter 10
Parker Davidson

Parker stepped onto the back porch, the morning air heavy with the damp scent of Nashville's soil. The garden patch he'd scratched out days ago, tucked against the fence, showed signs of life—tiny green sprouts of beans and carrots pushing through the dirt like stubborn promises. He smiled, a rare flicker of pride cutting through the weight of the past week.

The watering can in the garage was empty, so he grabbed the last bucket of rainwater, its surface rippling with each step. They had water bottles stashed in the basement for drinking and cooking, but he wanted to save those, using rainwater for the plants and odd chores. He poured carefully, the water soaking into the soil, then paused to inspect the sprouts again. They were small but strong, a quiet victory in a world turned upside down.

In the garage, he rummaged through the gardening shelves, pushing aside rusted tools and a bag of potting soil to find a container of fertilizer. The label was faded, but it'd do. Back at the garden, he sprinkled the gritty powder over the sprouts, then added another splash of water to work it into the earth.

Overhead, storm clouds churned, dark and swollen, their edges glowing faintly with the morning sun. Parker hurried around the house, checking the buckets he'd placed under the gutters. Most were half-full, so he swapped them out for spares from the garage, their metal rims cold against his hands. As he lowered the garage door, a soft patter of rain began, drops tapping the roof like a metronome.

"Just in time," he muttered, brushing dirt from his palms.

Inside, the house smelled of old wood and candle wax. Sydney lounged on the couch, her nose buried in a dog-eared paperback, her legs curled under a worn blanket. The sight of her, calm amidst the chaos, eased the knot in Parker's chest.

"Good book?" he asked, leaning against the doorframe.

She jumped, her bookmark slipping to the floor. "Geez, Parker, warn a girl." She grinned, holding up the book—a weathered mystery novel. "It's good. Might finish it today and start the next one."

"Hope so," he said, heading to his bedroom. "Don't read all our entertainment in one go."

He flopped onto his bed, the springs creaking, and cracked open his own book, a sci-fi novel his mom had recommended last summer. The words blurred as his mind wandered to her—where was she now? Wyoming, maybe, like Preston had said. He'd read two chapters, the rain now a steady drum against the windows, when the radio on his nightstand beeped, sharp and insistent. He marked his page, heart quickening, and grabbed it as he jogged to the kitchen.

"Parker, we've got a truck coming up the street from the south," Preston's voice crackled through, tense but controlled. "Quarter mile out, maybe. Unknown origin."

"Got it," Parker replied, moving to the front window. Rain streaked the glass, blurring the view, but he spotted the truck's outline. "I see it."

"Any idea who it is?" Preston asked, Bella's giggle faint in the background, a stark contrast to the tension in his voice.

"No clue," Parker said, squinting. "It's pulling into my driveway."

"Need me over there?" Preston's tone sharpened, urgent.

"Nah, let me check it out," Parker said, already moving to his room. He grabbed his pistol from the dresser, checking the magazine with practiced ease—his mom's drills echoing in his mind. "I'm good."

"I'm ready if you need me," Leo chimed in, his voice steady over the radio.

"Thanks, but I've got this," Parker said, clipping the radio to his pocket. He turned it off, the silence heavy as he peered through the window again. The truck's tinted windows hid its occupants, the rain making it impossible to see details. Two figures moved inside, shadowy and indistinct. His pulse thudded as the driver's door opened, a figure stepping out into the storm.

"Parker!" a voice called, sharp and achingly familiar.

He froze, his breath catching. "Mom?"

Kelsey sprinted through the rain, her jacket soaked, her face alight with relief. She crashed into him on the porch, wrapping him in a hug so tight it squeezed the air from his lungs.

"You're alright," she whispered, her voice thick with emotion.

Parker clung to her, his eyes stinging. "It's been crazy, Mom." He pulled back, and noticed a woman climbing out of the truck's passenger seat, blinking groggily. "Who's she?"

Kelsey turned, her arm still around him. "Anna, this is my son, Parker. Parker, Anna—she hitched a ride with me from Washington."

"Where are we?" Anna asked, her voice hoarse, a bandage stark against her forehead.

"Nashville," Parker said, grabbing Anna's backpack from the truck's backseat. "Let's get inside, out of this rain."

"Agreed," Kelsey said, guiding Anna toward the door, her hand steady on her shoulder.

Inside, Parker locked the door, the click grounding him. He grabbed the radio.

"Preston, false alarm. It's my mom." He switched it off before anyone could reply, catching Kelsey's raised eyebrow as she peeled off her wet jacket.

"Working radio?" she asked, kicking off her muddy boots. "How?"

"Preston had a Faraday cage," Parker said, setting Anna's backpack by the couch. "Kept some gear safe— radios, a couple flashlights."

They settled in the living room, the couch sagging under their weight. Sydney joined them, closing her book with a soft thud.

The rain battered the windows as they traded stories—Kelsey's grueling trek across the country, dodging looters and bartering for rides; Parker's days fortifying the house, planting the garden, and helping Preston.

Anna listened quietly, her eyes heavy but attentive, while Sydney chimed in with their own close calls. An hour later, the stories tapered off, and the rain slowed to a drizzle. Nala barked at the back door, her tail wagging furiously.

Sydney stood to let her out, then paused. "So, Anna, where you headed next?"

"Georgia, hopefully," Anna said, rubbing her bandaged forehead. "But I need a few days to rest. That trip was brutal."

"Want a doctor to check that wound?" Parker asked, nodding at her bandage.

Anna glanced at Kelsey, then back at him. "You've got a doctor here?"

"Across the street," Parker said. "Preston's friend, Chris. We moved him closer yesterday."

"That'd be great," Anna said, her shoulders relaxing.

Kelsey leaned forward, her eyes softening as she looked at Parker. "I was so worried about you, but you're handling this like a pro. The garden, the radio, keeping things together—I'm proud."

Parker's cheeks warmed, a grin tugging at his lips. "Thanks, Mom. Preston's been a huge help. And, uh, we've got some cash, too."

Kelsey's brow furrowed. "Cash? Isn't it worthless now?"

"Not here," Parker said, leaning back. "We hit the bank, pulled out half my account—about ten grand.

They're still using printed records, so it worked. Figured we'd stock up before trading becomes the only way."

Kelsey tilted her head, considering. "Smart. Might be worth grabbing more if things hold steady."

"The mayor's keeping things tight," Parker said. "Police are still patrolling, trying to hold the peace. It's not perfect, but it's not chaos yet."

Kelsey nodded, impressed. "Didn't expect that. Thought Nashville would've gone wild by now."

"I'll call Chris over to check Anna's head," Parker said, grabbing the radio. He clicked it on. "Chris, you there? Need you at my place with your medical bag."

"On my way," Chris replied, Preston's voice echoing in the background. "I'm coming, too."

"Thanks," Parker said, switching off the radio. He glanced at Kelsey. "You're gonna like Chris. He's solid."

Kelsey smirked, ruffling his hair. "Can't believe you're running the show here. I'm proud, kid."

Parker ducked her hand, grinning, and opened the back door to let Nala inside. She bounded inside, shaking rain from her fur, and Kelsey laughed, noticing the chicken coop through the window. "What's that?"

"Built it a few days ago," Parker said. "Figured fresh eggs would be nice. Got a few chickens from Preston."

Kelsey's eyes crinkled with approval. "Smart."

Parker stepped outside to check the rain buckets, now brimming with water. He swapped them for empties from the garage, the cold metal slick in his hands, and carried the full ones to the garage for safekeeping. By the time he finished, Chris and Preston were crossing the street, Chris with his medical bag, Preston with Bella trailing behind, her raincoat bright yellow against the gray day.

"Parker!" Preston called. "Can I grab one of those buckets for my chickens?"

"Take your pick," Parker said, gesturing to the garage. "Got four full ones, plus whatever's collecting now."

Chris knelt in front of Anna, setting his bag on the coffee table. He peeled back her bandage, his movements gentle but precise.

"Looks okay," he said, squinting at the wound. "Minor infection, nothing serious."

He pulled an alcohol wipe from his bag, cleaning the area with light dabs. Anna winced, her teeth gritted, but stayed still. Chris taped fresh gauze over the wound and handed her a small pill bottle. "Antibiotics. One twice a day for three days. You'll be fine."

"Thanks," Anna said, clutching the bottle. "Feels better knowing a doctor's checked it."

Kelsey rolled her eyes playfully. "Told you it wasn't that bad."

Preston laughed, settling into a chair. "How was your walk home, Kelsey? Long haul from Washington."

"Longer than yours," she teased, her smile warm. "Good to see you're keeping Parker in line."

"He's a sharp kid," Preston said, nodding at Parker. "Been a lifesaver these past few days."

Kelsey leaned back, her legs aching from the road. "I can see that."

Preston turned to Parker, his tone shifting. "You thought about hitting the gun store? We're low on ammo."

"Yeah, been meaning to," Parker said, scratching his neck. "You want to go now?"

"Could be fun," Preston said, a glint in his eye. "Need more nine-mil for my pistol, maybe some twenty-two for the rifle. Plus, who knows—might find something new."

Parker glanced at Kelsey. "Mom, you in?"

"Sure," she said, standing slowly. "Give me a minute to change out of these wet clothes. The less I sit around the less my legs hurt."

As she stepped away, Parker headed to the basement, grabbing a backpack stuffed with cash—nearly two thousand dollars left from the bank run. He slung it over his shoulder and rejoined Preston outside, where Kelsey was already waiting, her damp hair tied back.

"Where'd you get that truck?" Parker asked, nodding at the faded Chevy in the driveway.

"Nebraska. Guy traded it for some chores—fence work, chicken feeding."

"Nice," Parker said, running a hand over the Chevy's chipped paint. "We should keep it. Could be useful."

"My thoughts exactly," Kelsey said, settling into the passenger seat.

The group walked back across the street where Preston sent Bella inside to Angelina. While Parker set the buckets on the porch to be dealt with later. Preston twirled his keyring around his finger as he climbed into the driver's seat of his truck.

Preston started the engine, and they pulled out of the neighborhood, the streets slick with rain. Parker leaned forward from the back seat. "What'd you whisper to Sydney before we left, Mom?"

Kelsey smirked. "Told her to keep an eye on Anna. Don't know her well enough to trust her yet."

"Fair," Parker said, glancing out the window. "We almost there?"

"Another mile," Preston said, navigating a pothole. "Hope they've got ammo left. Should, if they're still open."

"Let's hope," Kelsey said, her hand resting on her own pistol.

They pulled into the gun store's parking lot, a squat brick building with barred windows, and what used to be a neon sign hanging high and proud above the building. Inside, the air was thick with the smell of gun oil and metal. Shelves lined with rifles and ammo boxes stretched to the back, surprisingly well-stocked. A burly man behind the counter, his beard streaked with gray, looked up. "How can I help you folks?"

"Looking for ammo," Preston said, leaning on the counter. "Nine-mil and twenty-two, mostly."

"Specifics?" the man asked, his eyes narrowing slightly.

"Ten boxes of each," Preston said. "If you've got it."

The man nodded, disappearing into a back room. Parker scanned the store, his gaze lingering on a display of tactical knives. Kelsey nudged him. "Eyes up. Don't get distracted."

The man returned with a heavy box, setting it on the counter with a thud. "Ten boxes each, like you asked. Five hundred dollars."

Parker's jaw dropped. "Five hundred? That's steep."

"Last ammo in the city," the man said, his tone flat. "Supply's tight. Price is what it is."

Kelsey's eyes narrowed, but she nodded. "Fair enough."

Parker knelt, pulling five hundred dollars from his backpack, the bills crinkled and damp. He handed them over, but the man's gaze lingered on the bag.

"Where'd a kid like you get that kind of cash?"

"None of your business," Parker said, his voice sharp as he lifted the ammo box.

The man's expression hardened. In a swift motion, he pulled a shotgun from under the counter, leveling it at them. "It's my business now."

Instinct kicked in. Parker, Kelsey, and Preston drew their pistols in unison, aiming at the man, the air crackling with tension. The standoff held, each second stretching taut, until the bell above the door jingled. A second man—tall, wiry, with a hunting rifle slung over his shoulder—stepped inside.

"What's going on here?" he barked, his eyes darting between them.

The store owner didn't flinch, but the newcomer raised his rifle, siding with him. Parker's heart pounded. Two against three, but the odds felt grim in the cramped store, with nowhere to take cover. His mind raced, searching for a way out. We talk, we die. We shoot, we might still die. He gripped his pistol tighter, glancing at Kelsey, whose steady gaze gave him a flicker of courage. This wasn't the end—not yet.

Chapter 11

Sydney Southerland

Sydney leaned back on the couch, the worn cushions sinking under her weight, the air in the Davidson living room thick with the lingering scent of rain and candle wax. Anna sat across from her, fidgeting with a Rubik's cube from the coffee table, its colors faded from years of use. The bandage on Anna's forehead stood out starkly, a reminder of the road's toll.

Sydney's book lay forgotten beside her, her thoughts drifting to Parker and Kelsey, still not back from the gun store. The quiet of the house felt heavy, broken only by the soft click of Anna's cube.

"So, how do you and Parker know each other?" Anna asked, her fingers twisting the cube with a restless rhythm.

Sydney offered a small smile. "We've been dating a couple years. Friends for a bit before that, but not long. We just... clicked, you know?" She paused, studying Anna's tired eyes. "What about you? Got family in Georgia, or is that just home?"

"Most of my family lives there," Anna said, setting the cube down with a soft thud. "Got friends there, too—

people I'd rather be with than stuck out here alone." She leaned forward, her voice dropping. "They're the kind who've been prepping for something like this forever. Stockpiles, generators, the works."

Sydney nodded, her fingers tracing the edge of the couch. "Makes sense, but getting there alone... it's risky. Things are getting worse out there—looters, fights. You saw what Kelsey dealt with."

Anna's jaw tightened, but she shrugged. "Worth the risk. Besides, I made it this far with Kelsey. I can handle a few more miles."

"When would you go?" Sydney asked, her voice soft but probing.

"Couple days, maybe," Anna said, rubbing her neck. "Need a break from walking. My legs feel like they're made of lead."

Sydney laughed, the sound lightening the room. "I wouldn't want to hike across the country either. You're tougher than you look."

Anna grinned, a flicker of pride in her eyes. Sydney stretched before grabbing her book from beside her, continuing where she had left off. She was a chapter in when she looked up, finding Anna asleep across the couch. Sydney stepped quietly past her, slipping on her shoes and heading out the front door. The air outside was cool, still heavy with the scent of rain-soaked asphalt. Across the street, Preston's house stood quiet, the truck nowhere in sight. She knocked, her knuckles sharp against the door.

Chris opened it, his stethoscope still around his neck, a tired smile on his face. "Hey, Sydney. What's up?"

"They're not back yet," she said, her voice tight. "Can

I use your radio to check on them?"

"Sure, come in," Chris said, stepping aside. "Watch your step—Bella's got toys everywhere."

Sydney chuckled, navigating a minefield of plastic blocks and stuffed animals scattered across the floor. "At least she's keeping busy."

In the dining room, a sturdy oak table held a radio, its antenna glinting in the dim light of a camping lantern. Chris picked it up, switching it on with a faint hum. "Hold this button and talk," he said, handing it to her.

Sydney pressed the button, her voice steady but edged with worry. "Parker, you guys okay? What's taking so long?" She paused, releasing the button, then tried again. "Parker, what's going on? Can you hear me?"

No response. The silence felt like a weight on her chest.

"If his radio's on, he should hear you," Chris said, leaning against the table. "Preston's always got his clipped to his belt."

"Why's there no static?" Sydney asked, setting the radio down, her fingers lingering on it.

"Fancy setting," Chris said. "Cuts the static, amplifies voices. Makes it easier to hear calls."

"Neat trick," Sydney said, but her mind was elsewhere. "I need to get back to make food. Let me know if you hear anything, okay?"

"Will do," Chris said. "Enjoy your dinner."

Sydney crossed the street, the damp air clinging to her skin. Back inside, she locked the door, finding Anna awake, sipping from a water bottle she'd grabbed from the kitchen. "Hungry?" Sydney asked, kicking off her shoes.

"Starving," Anna said, setting the bottle down. "Please, no more canned stuff."

Sydney grinned. "How's ramen sound? Nothing fancy, but better than beans."

"Perfect," Anna said, her voice brightening. "I'm over this post-EMP diet."

Sydney grabbed two packs of ramen from the pantry, their crinkly wrappers loud in the quiet house. She filled a pot with bottled water, setting it on the camp stove, the flame hissing softly.

"Hey, Anna, what day is it?" she asked, glancing over her shoulder.

Anna strolled across the room, ending at the calendar sitting on the wall, "May thirty-first?"

"Add three days, I haven't marked it in a bit. Been busy."

"It's the second." Anna replied, looking back at Sydney.

Sydney thought before looking back at her, "That means it's my eighteenth birthday!"

Anna's eyes widened. "No way! Happy birthday! My eighteenth was a blast—wish we could throw you a party."

Sydney laughed, stirring the ramen. "Thanks. Hold on—Parker's birthday is in a few days. He'll be eighteen, too." She paused, an idea sparking. "Wonder if we've got stuff for a cake."

Anna leaned forward, intrigued. "A cake? Without an oven?"

"I saw this thing online a while back," Sydney said, her voice quickening with excitement. "A solar oven. Uses the sun's heat to cook. Takes longer, but it works."

"That's real?" Anna asked, skeptical. "I thought that was just TV magic."

"Nope, it's legit," Sydney said. "You can use fire, too, but it's trickier to control. Wanna help make one tomorrow? We could do a double birthday thing—mine and Parker's."

"Love it," Anna said, clapping her hands. "What do we need?"

"Cardboard box, foil, tape, clear plastic wrap, and a skewer," Sydney listed, checking the pot. "We'll set it up at sunrise, let it cook all day."

"Deal," Anna said. "A cake's the least we deserve after this week."

Sydney rummaged through the kitchen drawers, pulling out a roll of foil and plastic wrap, while Anna hunted for tape and a sturdy box in the garage. They piled the supplies on the counter, ready for morning, then returned to the ramen. Sydney drained the pot, mixing in the seasoning, the savory smell filling the kitchen. She split the noodles into two bowls, handing one to Anna, and they sat at the dining table, eating in comfortable silence, the flickering candlelight casting soft shadows on the walls.

~

Parker Davidson

Parker's hand shook as he aimed his pistol at the gun store owner, the shotgun in the man's hands steady and menacing. Kelsey and Preston flanked him, their own guns drawn, the air thick with the smell of gun oil and tension. The second man, wiry and wild-eyed, stood by the door, his hunting rifle trained on them. Parker's mind raced, searching for a way out. Every option felt like a trap—talk too long, they'd lose the advantage; shoot first, they might not all walk away. His radio, clipped to his pocket, was still on from the last call, a mistake he hadn't noticed until Sydney's voice crackled through.

"Parker, you guys okay? What's taking so long?" A pause, then, "Parker, what's going on? Can you hear me?"

The sound was faint, but it sliced through the standoff like a blade. Both men's eyes snapped to Parker's pocket, their focus wavering. "Is that a working radio?" the store owner barked, his shotgun dipping slightly.

Parker cursed inwardly. He should've turned it off, but the radio's noise-canceling setting meant he hadn't noticed it was still active. Now it was a liability—more valuable to these men than the cash in his backpack.

"Yeah," he said, his voice steady despite the sweat beading on his forehead. "What's it to you?"

"How's it working?" the wiry man stammered, his rifle lowering an inch.

"None of your business," Parker snapped, seizing the moment. "Now!"

He ducked, firing at the store owner's arm, the shot echoing in the cramped space. Kelsey fired simultaneously, her bullet catching the man by the door in the shoulder. He crumpled with a grunt, his rifle clattering to the floor. The owner's shotgun roared, the blast wild and missing them entirely, pellets peppering a display case. Parker's second shot caught the owner in the skull, and he dropped, blood pooling on the hard carpet floor.

"We need to move," Parker said, holstering his pistol, his heart pounding. "Cops'll be here any second."

"Wait," Preston said, grabbing the ammo box from the counter. "Grab more while we're here."

Parker nodded, sprinting to the back room. Shelves towered with boxes of ammo, untouched by looters. He grabbed a box of *9mm*—1,000 rounds, the label read—and another of *.22* caliber, same count. The weight strained his arms as he hauled them to the truck, tossing them into the backseat beside Kelsey. Preston floored the gas, the tires squealing as they peeled out of the parking lot, the store's sign fading in the rearview mirror.

"Preston, take the box we paid for," Parker said, catching his breath. "It's got ten boxes of each, same as these."

"Thanks," Preston said, his voice tight. "We need to stash this quick. Cops see fresh ammo boxes, they'll know we were there."

Kelsey nodded, her face pale but composed. "Let's get home."

They pulled into the neighborhood, the familiar sight of Preston's house grounding Parker. Inside the Davidson home, the savory smell of ramen hit them like a wave of comfort. Sydney rushed over, throwing her arms around Parker.

"You didn't answer," she said, her voice muffled against his shoulder. "What happened?"

"Sorry," Parker said, hugging her back. "Guy at the gun store pulled a shotgun when he saw our cash. His buddy backed him up. Your radio call distracted them—gave us a chance to move."

Sydney pulled back, her eyes wide. "You're okay?"

"Yeah," Parker said, managing a smile. "Thanks to you."

Kelsey set the ammo boxes on the dining table, the thud heavy in the quiet room.

"Any ramen left?" she asked, brushing her damp hair back.

"I'll make more," Sydney said, heading to the kitchen. "You too, Parker?"

"Sure," he said, sinking onto the couch. "Need something to settle my nerves."

Kelsey's eyes lit up as she looked at the calendar. "Happy birthday, Sydney! Eighteen's a big one."

"Thanks," Sydney said, blushing. "Parker's is in a few days. He'll be eighteen, too."

Parker grinned, leaning back. "Sucks we can't throw a real party."

"Who says we can't?" Kelsey said, her tone playful. "No power doesn't mean no fun. We'll figure something out."

Sydney poured ramen into the pot, the water hissing as it boiled. "Speaking of fun," she said, leaning against the counter, "who's up for a board game tonight?"

"My feet are killing me, but a game might help," Kelsey said, kicking off her boots.

"My head's still throbbing," Anna added, rubbing her

bandage. "Count me in."

Parker stood, heading to the game shelf. He scanned the options—Monopoly, Scrabble, a beat-up box of Risk.

"Risk," he said, pulling it out. "Let's conquer the world."

He set up the board on the dining table, the colorful pieces a stark contrast to the day's chaos. Sydney brought two steaming bowls of ramen, setting them in front of Parker and Kelsey, the savory scent mixing with the faint smell of rain still clinging to their clothes. They ate quickly, the noodles warm and comforting, then dove into the game.

Sydney explained the rules to Anna, her voice animated as she described troop movements and alliances. Laughter filled the room as Parker's armies fell to Kelsey's ruthless strategy, and for a few hours, the world outside—its dangers, its uncertainties—faded into the background.

Chapter 12
Parker Davidson

Parker stirred as Sydney's gentle shake pulled him from sleep, her hand warm against his shoulder. The morning light filtered through the bedroom's cracked blinds, casting soft stripes across the quilt. He blinked, rolling over to meet her gaze, her eyes bright with a mix of mischief and warmth. "Good morning," he mumbled, his voice thick with sleep.

"Good morning, happy birthday!" She exclaimed.

Parker grinned, the weight of the milestone settling in. "Thanks. What's the plan today?"

She shrugged, stretching her arms. "You tell me. You've been the one running the show."

He chuckled, swinging his legs over the bed's edge, the cool hardwood grounding him. "Fair. Guess I'll start with the chickens—feed them, check their water."

He pulled on his jeans and a faded flannel, the fabric soft from years of wear, and grabbed his baseball cap from the dresser, settling it on his head.

As he stepped into the hallway, he nearly collided

with Anna, who was leaning against the wall, sipping from a water bottle.

"Morning, kid," she said, her voice rough from sleep, the bandage on her forehead slightly askew. "Happy birthday."

"Thanks," Parker said, sidestepping her. "Heading out to feed the chickens."

Nala bounded past him, her tail a blur as she darted for the back door. Parker followed, stepping onto the porch, the air crisp with the lingering damp of last night's rain.

The chicken coop stood sturdy against the fence, its wood weathered but solid. He grabbed a handful of feed from the bag atop the coop, the grain gritty between his fingers, and scattered it across the ground. The chickens clucked and scrambled, their feathers catching the morning light. He checked their water bowl, its surface rippling slightly—still half-full. Good enough for now. Nala sniffed at the coop, her nose twitching, before trotting back to his side.

Inside, the house smelled of coffee, a rare treat Kelsey must've brewed on the camp stove. She sat at the dining table, her hair pulled back, a mug cradled in her hands.

"Morning," she said, her eyes softening as she looked at him. "How's my birthday boy?"

"Tired but good," Parker said, grabbing a glass of water from the counter. "Chickens are fed. Thinking we hit the bank today, pull more cash just in case."

Kelsey nodded, setting her mug down with a soft clink. "Smart. What else?"

"Siphoning gas," Parker said, leaning against the counter. "We've got the new truck and Preston's across the street. If we stock up now, we won't be scrambling later."

"Good call," Kelsey said. "Where you planning to store it?"

"I've got an idea," Parker said, a spark of excitement in his voice. "Build a wooden stand in the garage, set a couple of fifty-five-gallon drums on it. Makes filling cans easier. We can do the same with water—use a hose to fill barrels, long enough to reach the front and back yards."

Kelsey's eyebrows lifted, impressed. "You've thought this through. Hardware store first, then?"

"Yup," Parker said. "Sydney, you in?"

Sydney poked her head in from the living room, her book tucked under her arm. "Sure, why not? Beats sitting around."

Kelsey turned to Anna, who was lingering by the doorway. "Anna, mind checking on Preston and Chris across the street? See if they need help with anything."

Anna nodded, grabbing her jacket. "On it."

They split off to get ready, Parker pulling on his boots and checking his pistol—habit now, after the gun store. He met Kelsey and Sydney by the front door, where Kelsey was slipping a knife into her belt. "We should grab some fence panels while we're at the store," Parker said, slinging his backpack over his shoulder.

Kelsey tilted her head, curious. "For what?"

"You'll see," Parker said with a grin, enjoying the mystery.

They piled into the Chevy, its engine coughing to life,

and drove to the hardware store, the streets quiet under a gray sky. The store was dim, lit only by skylights that cast a soft glow over aisles of tools and supplies. They navigated to the back, finding five fifty-five-gallon drums, their blue plastic gleaming faintly. On the way to the front, they grabbed a stack of fence panels. At the counter, a grizzled clerk tallied their haul.

"Two hundred," he said, his voice gruff, tired of still working.

Parker pulled two crumpled hundred-dollar bills from his pocket, handing them over. "Thanks."

"Have a good one," Sydney called as they hauled the supplies to the truck, the drums and panels barely fitting in the bed.

Back home, Kelsey headed inside while Parker and Sydney stayed in the garage. Parker measured the wood for the stand, marking it with a pencil, the graphite scratching softly. He showed Sydney how to use the saw, guiding her hands as she cut, her focus intense.

"Grandpa taught me this at his cabin," Parker said. "Summers out there, no grid, just us and the woods. He'd have loved this—figuring out how to make things work."

Sydney smiled, sawing steadily. "Sounds like he was cool."

"The best," Parker said, a pang of grief hitting him. He shook it off, helping her finish the cuts. They nailed the plywood top to the stand, its edges flush, and heaved a drum onto it. The stand held firm, low but sturdy, perfect for filling cans from the bottom. Parker shook the gas cans on the floor—empty, as expected. "We'll fill these as we siphon," he said.

Sydney nodded, wiping sweat from her brow. "I'll

make lunch. You keep at it."

Parker lined up the remaining drums along the garage's back wall, then poured the rainwater buckets into one, the water glugging until it reached halfway. He stepped inside, where Sydney was frying French toast on the camp stove, the sweet smell of eggs and bread filling the kitchen. She'd used the last of the loaf and the chickens' eggs, piling the golden slices on a plate. Parker grabbed a few, drizzling syrup, and sat at the table, the wood creaking under his elbows.

"What's next out there?" Kelsey asked, joining him with her own plate.

"Finishing the stand was step one," Parker said between bites. "Now I'm working on something with the fence panels. You'll like it."

Kelsey leaned forward, eyes narrowing playfully. "Spill it, Parker."

"Nope," he said, grinning. "It's a surprise."

She groaned, but her smile betrayed her amusement.

Parker finished eating, rinsed his plate with a splash of water, and headed back to the garage. Outside, a narrow gap ran between the garage and the property's fence, just wide enough for his plan. He measured it, then cut two six-foot 2x4s, nailing one to the garage's side and the other to the fence, four feet apart. A third board connected them at the top, forming a frame. He hauled a sheet of plywood over the top, nailing it down to create a roof, the hammer's rhythm steady in the quiet afternoon.

Next, he pried a board from a fence panel, exposing its 2x4 frame, and cut a smaller section to serve as a door. He attached it with hinges from a previous hardware run, the metal creaking as he tested it. Needing a break, he ducked inside for a water bottle, the cool liquid soothing his dry throat.

"Is it done?" Sydney asked, looking up from the couch, her book open on her lap.

"Almost," Parker said, wiping his mouth. "Just a few more touches."

"You're so secretive," she teased, her eyes bright.

"For good reason," he said, winking.

Back outside, he cut a small notch in the fence door's top, then nailed a scrap wood shelf inside the new enclosure. He connected a hose to the water-filled drum, threading it through the notch with a nozzle for control. Stepping back, he admired his work—a makeshift outdoor shower, simple but functional.

He gathered everyone outside, his chest swelling with pride. "Check it out," he said, gesturing to the enclosure. "It's a shower."

Sydney gasped, her hand flying to her mouth. "No way. You built this?"

Kelsey clapped his shoulder. "Not pretty, but it'll work. Well done."

"Can I go first?" Sydney asked, practically bouncing.

"Go for it," Parker and Kelsey said in unison.

"Anna and I caught a shower somewhere—Idaho, maybe Nebraska," Kelsey said, shrugging. "You need it more."

Sydney grabbed a change of clothes, her laughter echoing as she darted to the shower. Parker, Kelsey, and Anna headed inside, Nala trailing behind, her tail wagging.

Upstairs, Parker pulled Kelsey into his room, his stomach knotting with nerves. "Mom, I need to talk to you."

She leaned against the doorframe, her expression curious. "What's on your mind?"

Parker took a deep breath, his hands stuffed in his pockets. "I'm thinking about proposing to Sydney."

Kelsey's eyebrows shot up, but she stayed quiet, waiting for him to continue.

"We've been together four years," he said, his voice low but steady. "Everything that's happened—the EMP, all this chaos—it's made me realize I don't want to wait. I know it's fast, but it feels right."

Kelsey crossed her arms, studying him. "You've thought this through?"

"Yeah," he said, meeting her gaze. "I'm sure."

She nodded slowly, a small smile breaking through. "If it's what you want, I'm with you. Just make sure you're both ready."

"Thanks, Mom," Parker said, relief loosening his shoulders. He gave her a quick nod, then headed downstairs, his mind already on the next step.

Sydney stepped inside, her hair damp, a grin on her face. "That shower's a game-changer," she said. "Your turn?"

"Definitely," Parker said, grabbing clothes and a towel. The water was ice-cold, the pressure weak, but it washed away the sweat and grime, soothing his aching muscles. He dressed in the enclosure, the air cool against his skin, and draped his towel over a dining room chair inside.

He grabbed his backpack, slinging it over his shoulder. "Going for a walk," he said, heading for the door.

Sydney raised an eyebrow. "With your backpack?"

"Strength training," he lied, patting his shoulders. "Gotta stay fit."

"Uh-huh," Anna said, smirking. "Be safe."

Parker walked down the sidewalk, the neighborhood quiet. His destination was the pawn shop in the town's central lot, its jewelry case etched in his memory from a prior visit. He crossed the empty parking lot, the asphalt cracked and littered with debris, and stepped inside. The shop was deserted, its air heavy with dust. The jewelry case gleamed faintly, rings sparkling under a sliver of sunlight. He spotted a simple silver band with a small diamond, perfect for Sydney. He slipped it into its velvet box, tucking it into his pocket. A twinge of guilt hit him, stealing, but with no one around, he hesitated.

Two men approached as he stepped outside, their boots crunching on gravel.

"What'd you take?" one demanded, his hand resting on a knife sheathed at his back.

"You the owner?" Parker asked, his pulse quickening.

"Yeah," the man said, pulling the knife, its blade glinting. "What'd you grab?"

"Just a ring," Parker said, raising his hands. "I'll pay. Thought the place was abandoned."

"Seven-fifty," the second man barked. "Hand it over."

Parker pulled the cash from his pocket, counting out the bills. A police officer—Sergeant Harrison from the bank—watched from across the lot. Parker handed over the money, expecting the deal to close. But the owner's eyes narrowed. "Give me the ring back."

"I paid for it," Parker said, his voice steady but his hand inching toward his pistol.

"You stole it first," the man snarled, lunging with the knife.

Parker tried to dodge, but the blade sank into his right leg, pain exploding like fire. He stumbled, ripping his pistol from its holster and firing three shots into the man's chest. The second man raised his hands, but Parker shot twice, dropping him. Blood seeped from his leg, the knife still embedded, as he collapsed, screaming.

Sergeant Harrison sprinted over, kneeling beside him. "Parker, hang on. You know a doctor?"

"Chris," Parker gasped, pain blurring his vision. "My house. Take me there."

"You sure?" Harrison asked, skeptical.

"Yes!" Parker yelled, clutching his leg.

Harrison helped him up, supporting his weight as they staggered to the bank, where Sergeant Landon joined them. They half-carried Parker home, his leg throbbing with each step. He cursed himself for leaving the radio behind—no way to warn anyone. As they reached the driveway, Parker's leg buckled, and he fell, screaming as the knife shifted.

"Get them out here!" he gasped to Harrison, who bolted to the door.

Kelsey, Sydney, and Anna rushed out, Sydney's face

crumpling at the sight of the knife. Anna sprinted across the street for Chris and Preston.

Kelsey knelt beside Parker, her voice trembling. "Oh, my God, are you okay?"

Parker gritted his teeth, groaning.

Chris arrived, medical bag in hand, Preston and Anna behind him with extra supplies.

"You're in good hands, son," Chris said, kneeling. "I need to cut your pant leg to get to the wound."

Parker nodded, unable to speak. Chris pulled the ring box and holster from his pocket, tossing them aside. Sydney's eyes locked on the box, tears spilling over. Chris cut the pant leg, the scissors snipping loudly.

"This'll hurt," he said, handing Parker a cloth. "Bite this."

Parker clamped down as Chris yanked the knife free, pain searing through him like lightning. He wanted to scream, to lash out, but held still, the cloth muffling his groans.

Chris pressed gauze to the wound, blood soaking through instantly.

"Preston, hold pressure," he said, grabbing his suture kit.

Preston knelt, pressing hard, his face grim.

Chris stitched quickly, his hands steady, then wrapped the wound in fresh gauze, taping it securely.

"Take these," he said, handing Parker a pill bottle. "Strong painkillers. One every eight hours. Should help till tomorrow."

Parker swallowed the pills with a gulp of water, his

voice hoarse. "Thanks."

Kelsey and Chris helped him inside, settling him on his bed. Sydney gathered his things, the ring box clutched in her hand, her eyes questioning but silent. Parker's head swam, pain and exhaustion pulling him under. As he drifted off, the weight of the ring—and what it meant—lingered in his mind.

Chapter 13
Sydney Southerland

Sydney ate at her French toast, thinking about what had happened yesterday, the events replaying in her mind.

"Morning, Sydney," Anna called, stepping into the living room.

"Morning," Sydney replied, swallowing her last bite.

Anna sat across from her, her eyes gentle but probing. "How you holding up? Yesterday was rough."

Sydney sighed, pushing her plate aside. "I don't know. Seeing him like that—blood everywhere, the knife..." She paused, her fingers tracing the table's grain. "Then that ring box. It's just... a lot."

Anna leaned forward, her voice soft. "I get it. That's a wild mix of emotions. If you need to talk, I'm here."

"Thanks," Sydney said, managing a small smile. She grabbed her book from the coffee table, a worn mystery novel, and headed to the front porch. The rocking chair creaked as she settled in, the warm breeze carrying the scent of damp grass and distant woodsmoke. She read for a while, the words blurring as her thoughts drifted back to Parker, but thirst pulled her inside. She grabbed a water bottle from the kitchen, its plastic cool against her palm, and returned to the porch, savoring the quiet for an hour before heading back in.

Kelsey was awake now, stirring coffee on the camp stove, her expression warm but tired. "Morning, Sydney. You okay?"

Sydney shrugged, leaning against the counter. "Not sure. Yesterday's still sinking in. I don't know what to feel."

Kelsey nodded, setting her mug down with a soft clink. "That's normal. It was a lot to take in. But don't let it hold you back—keep moving forward."

"You're right," Sydney said, straightening. "I'm gonna feed the chickens."

Sydney grabbed the feed bag from next to the back door as she stepped outside. She mozied over to the chicken coop, dodging them all one by one. She scattered feed from the bag, the chickens clucking eagerly, and refilled their water bowl with the hose, the water glugging softly. Back inside, she found Preston waiting, his flannel rumpled, a determined look in his eyes.

"Hey, Sydney," he said, leaning against the wall. "Could use your help today if you're up for it."

"What's up?" she asked, shutting the back door, the latch clicking.

"Chris and I were talking about our cabin out east. It's got food, supplies, maybe some ammo. We want to grab it before someone else does."

Sydney nodded, her interest piqued. A trip might clear her head. "Sure, I'll get dressed. Be right out."

"We'll be in the truck," Preston said, heading out.

Sydney slipped into Parker's room, careful not to disturb him, and grabbed a change of clothes from her bag. In the bathroom, she changed into jeans and a hoodie, the fabric soft but practical. She grabbed her pistol from the kitchen counter, checking the magazine out of habit, and headed outside. "I'll be back later," she called.

"Be safe," Kelsey replied, her voice muffled as the door shut.

Across the street, Preston's truck idled, its engine a low rumble. Sydney climbed into the backseat, and Preston pulled out, the neighborhood fading behind them. They hit the highway, the road littered with stalled cars, their hoods rusted and windows shattered. Sydney hadn't seen the highway since the EMP hit and the eerie stillness—broken only by the occasional abandoned suitcase or bicycle—sent a chill through her. They drove for nearly two hours, weaving around wrecks, before exiting onto a cracked paved road that gave way to a dusty dirt path. The truck bumped along until a small cabin emerged, its log walls weathered but solid, nestled among pines.

Preston killed the engine and they stepped out, the air sharp with the scent of sap and earth. The cabin's interior was dim, but sunlight streamed through wide windows, illuminating dust motes in the air.

"Three rooms and a shed out back," Preston said, scanning the space. "Let's clear it first."

Sydney nodded. "I'll start in the kitchen."

"Chris and I'll take the bedroom," Preston said. "Ammo and tools in there."

Sydney crossed to the kitchen, her boots echoing on the hardwood. Out of habit, she flicked the light switch, expecting nothing. The bulb flared to life, casting a warm glow. She froze, heart racing. "Preston!"

He jogged in, eyes wide. "What's wrong?"

She flipped the switch again, the light blinking on. "Check this out."

Preston's jaw dropped. "No way. The solar panels on the roof still work?"

"Guess so," Sydney said, turning the light off. "But the batteries are probably shot, so it's daytime only."

"Still," Preston said, grinning. "We're taking them. Can't leave that behind."

Sydney nodded. "Let's grab them first, stack everything else on top."

"Chris!" Preston called. "Get in here."

Chris appeared, wiping his hands on his jeans. "What's up?"

"Sydney found that the solar panels still work," Preston said. "We're starting with those."

"Nice," Chris said, heading outside. "Ladder's on the side from last season's repairs."

They set up the ladder, its metal rungs cold under Sydney's hands. Preston climbed onto the roof, his boots scraping the shingles. "Need a screwdriver," he called.

Sydney darted into the bedroom, spotting a toolbox on the bed, its lid rusted. She grabbed a screwdriver and tossed it up to Preston, who caught it with a fumble. He worked quickly, unbolting the panels and handing them down to Sydney and Chris, who stacked them carefully in the truck's bed.

With the panels secured, they returned to the cabin, packing canned goods, tools, and boxes of ammo—*9mm* and *.22*, by the labels. The work took two hours, the truck's bed nearly overflowing, cargo spilling over the cab. Preston grabbed ratchet straps from the backseat, their nylon edges frayed, and secured the load with sharp tugs.

As they hit the paved road back to the highway, Sydney spotted a group of people trudging up an on-ramp, their faces gaunt, bags slung over their shoulders. Preston slowed, his hands tightening on the wheel, but he shook his head. "Better not stop. Could go south fast."

Sydney nodded, her gaze drifting out the window. Her thoughts circled back to the ring box.

"Hey, Preston," she said, her voice low. "Yesterday, when Chris pulled stuff from Parker's pockets, there was a ring box. Any idea what it was for?"

Preston and Chris exchanged a quick glance, their expressions guarded. "He didn't say anything to me," Preston said, his tone careful. "We were with him most of the day, but not when he went out."

Sydney frowned, unconvinced, but let it drop. The drive back was quiet, the hum of the engine filling the silence. They pulled into the driveway, the familiar sight of the neighborhood bringing her back to reality.

"Need help unloading?" she asked.

"Nah, we've got it," Chris said, hopping out. "Thanks for coming along."

"Anytime," Sydney said, managing a smile. "Needed the break."

~

Preston Sanchez

Preston popped the tailgate, the metal groaning, and loosened the ratchet straps, their nylon edges fraying further with each tug. He and Chris began unloading, stacking cans and tools in the garage, the solar panels leaning against the wall like trophies. The air smelled of dust and gasoline, the afternoon sun casting long shadows across the driveway.

"Did you know about the ring box?" Preston asked, keeping his voice low as he handed Chris a box of ammo.

Chris shook his head, setting the box down. "Not a clue. I didn't even know he'd left until he came back stabbed."

Preston frowned, glancing toward Parker's house. "Kelsey might know something. If Parker's keeping it quiet, we shouldn't ruin it."

"Agreed," Chris said, lifting a solar panel. "Sydney saw the box, though. So did everyone else. She's probably got questions."

"Let's keep it under wraps for now," Preston said. "If she's piecing it together, that's Parker's to handle."

They finished unloading, the garage now a maze of supplies, and closed the door with a heavy thud. Inside, they sank onto the couch, the cushions sagging under their weight.

"Should we tell Leo about yesterday?" Chris asked, stretching his arms. "He'll notice the blood in their driveway."

Preston shook his head. "Let Parker decide what to share. Kid's got enough on his plate."

Chris nodded, then perked up. "You know Parker—he'll want to work through the pain. I've got crutches at the clinic. Could grab them for him."

"Good call," Preston said. "Let's make it quick. Don't need trouble."

They climbed back into the truck, the engine rumbling to life, and drove to Chris's clinic across town. The building loomed, its front windows shattered, pill bottles and broken glass littering the sidewalk—looters, probably after meds. Preston kept the truck idling, his eyes scanning the street, while Chris darted inside. He returned minutes later, tossing a pair of aluminum crutches into the bed, their clatter sharp in the quiet.

They drove back, parking in Preston's driveway, and crossed to Parker's house. Sydney answered the door, her hair still damp from the shower.

"Hey. Come on in," she said, stepping aside.

"Thanks," Chris said. "Where's Parker?"

"In the living room," Parker called, his voice strained but steady.

"Mind if I check your leg?" Chris asked, setting his medical bag down.

"Go for it," Parker said, propping himself up on the couch. "Was gonna ask you to anyway."

Chris knelt, peeling back the bandage, the wound red but clean.

"Healing okay," he said, re-wrapping it. "Brought you these." He handed Parker the crutches, their rubber tips scuffed but sturdy.

"Thanks," Parker said, testing them with a wince.

Preston stepped onto the porch with Kelsey, the air cool against his skin.

"So, that ring box yesterday," he said, cutting to the chase. "You know anything about it?"

Kelsey glanced around, her voice low. "Parker pulled me aside yesterday. Said he wants to propose to Sydney. I'm guessing he was getting the ring when it all went down."

Preston nodded, relief flickering. "That's what we figured. Sydney asked about it on the drive back. We didn't say anything."

"Good," Kelsey said, her eyes softening. "She's probably got an idea, but let's keep it quiet. It's Parker's moment."

They stepped back inside, where Chris was showing Parker how to balance on the crutches.

"Takes practice," Chris said. "Once you're walking without them, you'll be a pro."

Parker laughed, a hint of his usual spark returning. "Heard that's how it goes. How long till I'm back on my feet?"

"Few days to a few weeks," Chris said, packing his bag. "Depends on the damage, but it's hard to tell without scans. Just take it easy."

"Will do," Parker said, though his tone suggested otherwise.

"We should head back," Chris said, standing. "Dinner's probably ready."

"Thanks again," Parker said, leaning on the crutches.

Preston and Chris crossed the street, the fading light casting their shadows long.

"So, Kelsey knew," Preston said, opening his front door. "Parker's planning to propose."

Chris nodded. "Let's keep it from Sydney. Easy enough."

"Where were you guys?" Angelina called from the kitchen, the savory smell of stew wafting through the house.

"Checking on Parker," Preston said, grabbing bowls from the cabinet, their ceramic edges chipped. "Talked to Kelsey."

"Everything okay?" Angelina asked, stirring a pot on the camp stove.

"Yeah," Preston said. "Go get Bella for dinner?"

"She's upstairs playing," Angelina said.

Preston climbed the stairs, the wood creaking under his boots.

"Bella, dinner's ready," he called.

"Okay!" she chirped, dancing down the stairs, her head nodding to a tune she was humming.

At the dining table, Angelina set out bowls of stew, steam curling upward. They held hands, Bella's small fingers warm in Preston's, and said grace, the words a quiet anchor in the fading light.

Chapter 14
Parker Davidson

Parker jolted awake, his heart pounding from a nightmare he couldn't quite grasp—shadowy figures, gunfire, Sydney's voice calling his name. The room was dark, the air heavy with the faint smell of candle wax and old wood. His throat felt like sandpaper.

He reached for his crutches propped against the nightstand, and winced as he swung his legs over the bed's edge. His injured leg throbbed, a dull reminder of the knife. Forgetting his condition for a moment, he set his foot down, and a sharp spasm shot through him, electric and unforgiving. He yanked it back, biting back a groan, and leaned against the headboard, catching his breath.

He hobbled to the kitchen, the crutches' rubber tips squeaking on the hardwood. Grabbing a water bottle from the counter, he leaned against it, the cool plastic soothing his palm. He took a sip, the water cold against his dry throat, then capped it and made his way back to his room.

But sleep wouldn't come. It never did once he was

up—his mind too restless, replaying the chaos of the past days. With a sigh, he grabbed his crutches and water and shuffled to the living room, the house silent except for the faint creak of the floorboards.

He flopped onto the couch, its springs groaning, and picked up a book from the coffee table—a worn guide to surviving Tennessee's wilderness. He lit the candle on the side table and peeled open the book's cover. Its pages detailed edible plants, trapping techniques, and hunting tips, the text dense but practical. Parker's eyes lingered on a section about wild berries, his mind drifting to the forest just beyond the neighborhood.

An idea sparked: the forest could be the perfect place to propose to Sydney. Quiet, private, a world away from the EMP's chaos. He imagined her smile, the way her eyes lit up when she was surprised, and his chest tightened with nervous anticipation.

He read until dawn, the sky outside shifting from black to soft gray, the words blurring as his thoughts circled the ring box hidden in the kitchen. Sydney's footsteps stirred in the bedroom, and he set the book down, grabbing his crutches to meet her.

He leaned against the doorway, watching her stretch, her hair a messy cascade.

"Morning," he said, his voice low, startling her.

She jumped, then laughed. "Geez, Parker. You're up early. Shouldn't you be resting?"

"Couldn't sleep," he said, shrugging. "Rather be doing something."

She raised an eyebrow, pulling on a hoodie. "Did you at least make coffee?"

"Nope," he said, a grin tugging at his lips. "Waiting for you. Otherwise, I'd drink it all."

"Fair," she said, tying her shoes. "What's the plan today?"

"Thought we could walk through the forest," he said, his heart picking up speed. "Get some air. I also want to see what plants are out there. This book has me curious."

"Sounds good," she said, her eyes brightening. "Let's go soon, before it gets too hot."

They dressed quickly, Parker pulling on jeans and a flannel, careful not to jostle his leg. In the dining room, they grabbed their pistols from the table. Parker slipped the ring box into his pocket when Sydney's back was turned, his fingers brushing the velvet, nerves tingling. He clipped the radio to his belt, its weight reassuring.

As they headed for the door, Sydney paused. "Should we leave a note for your mom and Anna?"

"Good call," Parker said, leaning on his crutches. "You want to write it? I'll wait."

Sydney nodded, grabbing a notepad from the kitchen. She scribbled a quick message—*Gone to the forest. Back later. -Sydney*—and rejoined him. "All set."

She held the door open, and Parker navigated the porch steps, his crutches sinking slightly into the damp grass at the bottom. Sydney followed, her steps light but close, ready to steady him if needed. They walked down the sidewalk, the neighborhood quiet. The forest's edge loomed just beyond the last houses, its dirt trails winding through towering pines and oaks. They stepped onto the path, the ground soft underfoot, the air cool and thick with the scent of moss and earth.

"What do you think the future's gonna look like?" Sydney asked, her voice cutting through the rustle of leaves.

Parker adjusted his grip on the crutches, thinking. "A lot of fighting at first. People scrambling for what's left. But after that—maybe some peace. Rebuilding. Once folks figure out how to stand on their own, they'll see they need to work together."

Sydney nodded, her gaze distant. "The fighting's what worries me."

"Yeah," Parker said, his voice softening. "But it won't last forever. Once resources aren't so tight, people won't have as much to fight over."

"I hope so," she said, then stopped, her eyes catching something. "Look," she whispered, pointing. "Deer."

Parker turned, spotting two does grazing in a clearing, their ears twitching. "Haven't seen those around here in ages," he said, his voice low.

Sydney watched them, her face softening, the morning light catching her profile. Parker's heart thudded. This was it.

He maneuvered behind her, awkward on his crutches, and lowered himself to one knee, pain shooting through his leg but ignored. He pulled the ring box from his pocket, his fingers trembling as he opened it, the silver band glinting faintly.

"Sydney," he said, his voice steady despite the nerves knotting his stomach. "We've been through a lot—four years, now this EMP. It's made me realize I don't want to wait anymore. I want us to face whatever comes next together. Will you marry me?"

She turned, her eyes widening, then softening as she saw the ring. Her hand flew to her mouth, and for a moment, the forest seemed to hold its breath.

~

Kelsey Davidson

Kelsey stirred as Anna's voice broke through her sleep, the bed creaking as she sat up. "Hey, I made eggs," Anna said, standing in the doorway. "Want some?"

Kelsey rubbed her eyes, the room still dim. "Eggs? Yeah, I'm in. Give me a minute."

Anna nodded and headed downstairs, her footsteps fading. Kelsey swung her legs out of bed, the cool floor grounding her as she pulled on jeans and a sweater.

The house smelled of sizzling eggs and coffee, a rare comfort in the post-EMP world. Downstairs, Anna sat at the dining table, two plates of scrambled eggs waiting, their golden hue flecked with herbs. Kelsey took a seat, the chair creaking, and dug in, the eggs savory and rich.

"These are incredible," she said, savoring a bite. "Where'd you learn to cook like this?"

Anna shrugged, poking at her plate. "Back in Georgia, my mom taught me. She was big on cooking from scratch. I'm not huge on it, but I picked up a few tricks."

Kelsey nodded, finishing her plate and carrying it to the kitchen. A scrap of paper on the counter caught her eye—Sydney's note. *Gone to the forest. Back later. - Sydney.* She set it down, frowning.

"Didn't even hear them leave," she said, glancing at

Anna.

"Yeah, saw the note earlier," Anna said, leaning back. "Figured they're fine. Probably just needed some air."

Kelsey's lips quirked. "Hope so."

She turned to Anna, her tone shifting. "So, when are you thinking of heading to Georgia?"

Anna's gaze drifted to the window, her fingers tapping the table. "Soon, maybe a couple days. My parents are out there alone. They're tough, but they could use help."

"We can put together a pack for you," Kelsey said, leaning against the counter. "Food, water, some supplies from us and Preston's place. Make sure you've got enough to get there safely."

Anna's shoulders relaxed, a grateful smile breaking through. "That'd be a huge help. What I've got now wouldn't last the trip."

"We'll start today," Kelsey said. "Get it ready so you can leave when you're set."

A knock at the door sent Nala into a frenzy, her barks echoing through the house. Kelsey crossed to the door, finding Preston on the porch, his flannel streaked with dirt.

"Morning," he said. "Got any seed packets? We need to start planting. Should've done it sooner."

"Yeah, we've got plenty," Kelsey said, leading him to the garage. She pulled a plastic bin from a shelf, its lid dusty, filled with packets of beans, tomatoes, and squash. "Take what you need. We've got more downstairs—used to stock up when they went on sale."

Preston's eyes lit up. "Perfect. Meant to grab some

before the EMP, but the stores are probably cleaned out now."

"Take the whole bin," Kelsey said, handing it to him. "Bring it back when you're done. I need to help Anna with getting a pack together for her trip home."

"Appreciate it," Preston said, hefting the bin. "I'll get these planted—Bella'll love digging in the dirt. If you need anything for Anna, I'd be happy to pitch in."

"That'd be great," Kelsey said.

"Got it," Preston said.

"Could I get a radio? Parker has the other one. If it's no trouble."

"I'll bring it with the seeds," Preston said, heading out. "Oh, and that shower Parker built—mind if I use it sometime?"

Kelsey laughed. "Sure, but we're low on water. Running on rainwater for now."

"Still a game-changer," Preston said, grinning as he left.

Kelsey shut the door, the latch clicking, and turned to Anna, who was flipping through a book on the couch. "Ready to start on your pack?"

Anna set the book down, nodding. "Yeah. What should we put in it?"

"Food, water, a small medical kit," Kelsey said, ticking off items on her fingers. "A sleeping bag, maybe some tools. Basics to get you to Georgia."

"You got a sleeping bag I can use?" Anna asked.

"Yup," Kelsey said. "We've got one in the basement. And a backpack to hold everything—your trip's not too far, so it shouldn't be too heavy."

They headed downstairs, the air cool and musty, the darkness broken only by a flashlight's beam. They gathered a sleeping bag, canned goods, a first-aid kit, and a multi-tool, hauling it all upstairs. Kelsey packed the backpack methodically—sleeping bag at the bottom, food and water in the main compartment, medical kit and smaller items in the side pockets. "Wash your clothes before you go," she said. "Start fresh."

Anna nodded, her eyes grateful. "Thanks, Kelsey. This means a lot."

Kelsey excused herself, heading to the outdoor shower. The water was cold, the pressure weak, but it washed away the grime, leaving her refreshed. She dried off, her thoughts drifting to Parker and Sydney, hoping their walk was the escape they needed.

Chapter 15

Parker Davidson

Sydney's eyes glistened, her breath catching as she turned to face Parker, the silver ring gleaming in the forest's dappled light.

"Yes," she said, her voice trembling with joy, barely above a whisper. She stepped closer, her hands shaking as she reached for him.

Parker fumbled with the ring box, his fingers clumsy from nerves and the ache in his leg. He slid the simple silver band onto her finger, its small diamond catching the sunlight. Using his crutches for balance, he stood, pulling her into a kiss.

He stepped back, a sheepish grin spreading across his face. "So... did you know I was gonna do this?"

Sydney laughed, wiping her eyes. "I had a hunch. That ring box in your pocket—after the stabbing? Kind of gave it away. But I didn't want to ruin it."

Parker chuckled, shaking his head. "Yeah, I should've hidden it better. Or, you know, not gotten stabbed."

She leaned in, kissing him again. They continued down the dirt trail, pine needles crunching underfoot, the forest alive with birdsong and the rustle of leaves.

Sydney kept glancing at the ring, her fingers twisting it as they walked. When they reached a fork in the path, they turned back, the journey home stretching over a couple of hours. The sun climbed higher, warming the air, and Parker's leg throbbed with each step.

Back in the neighborhood, they wound through quiet streets, the asphalt cracked and littered with debris. Parker unlocked the front door, the hinges creaking, and they stepped inside, the house cool and dim. Sydney flopped onto the couch, her boots dangling over the armrest, the ring catching the light from a nearby window.

Parker watched her, wondering if she'd say anything about the proposal. She seemed to be waiting, a playful glint in her eyes, as if testing whether Kelsey or Anna would notice the ring first.

He hobbled to the kitchen, grabbing a granola bar from a dwindling stash, the wrapper crinkling as he tore it open. He sank into an armchair, the springs groaning, and munched in silence, his thoughts swirling between the proposal and the lingering pain in his leg.

Kelsey entered, her hair damp from the shower, the faint scent of soap trailing her.

"Hey, you're back," she said, settling at the dining table. "How was the walk?"

"Needed to stretch my legs," Parker said, adjusting his crutches. "Thought some air might help the healing."

"Hope it does," Kelsey said, her eyes soft with concern. "Get better soon."

"Don't we all," Parker said, managing a smile. "Where's Anna?"

"Showering," Kelsey replied. "She's planning to leave tomorrow. We put together a pack for her—food, water, medical kit, sleeping bag. Should be enough for Georgia."

"That's where she's headed?" Parker asked, leaning forward.

"Yeah," Kelsey said. "It's not far. Should be manageable."

Sydney looked up from the couch. "How's her head doing?"

"Looks good," Kelsey said. "No bandage anymore, and the cut's closed up. She'll be fine."

Parker nodded, then hesitated, his mind shifting to a nagging worry. "Mom, what's the deal with those warships on the coast? I remember the news mentioning them before the EMP."

Kelsey's face tightened, her fingers tapping the table. "When Anna and I were traveling here, we heard rumors. The ships were getting closer—too close. Makes me think the EMP was meant to soften us up for an invasion."

Parker's stomach sank. "If they hit the coast and the states there can't stop them, they'll push inland. Nashville's not that far."

"Exactly," Kelsey said, her voice low. "But organizing a defense? Without comms, it'd take days to rally people for one city, weeks for a state. We're scattered."

"We can't just sit here," Parker said, his jaw tightening. "I'm not letting some invaders take what's ours."

"Something will come together. Maybe NATO's

watching, or someone's organizing out there. But for now, we wait and prepare," Sydney said.

Parker sighed. "Hope it doesn't get worse."

"We'll deal with it," Sydney said, her voice firm. "One step at a time."

He grabbed his wilderness survival book, its pages worn from late-night reading, and flipped to where he'd left off, diving into a section on trapping small game.

Anna emerged from the backyard, her hair wet, a towel draped over her shoulders. "Hey, guys," she said, her voice bright. "How was the walk?"

"Pretty good," Sydney said, sitting up. "Saw some deer, nothing crazy."

Anna nodded, then glanced at Parker. "How's the leg?"

He looked up, startled from his book. "Better. Still hurts, but I haven't checked it. Feels like it's healing."

"Good," Anna said, heading upstairs. "Hope it's back to normal soon."

Parker finished the book's final page, the words blurring as his eyes grew heavy. He set it down, intending to grab water, but Sydney stopped him. "What do you need?"

"Just water," he said, leaning back. "I can get it."

"Nope," she said, hopping up. She returned with two bottles, handing him one before curling up on the couch. She quickly fell asleep.

Parker sipped his water, the cool liquid soothing, and soon drifted off, the day's fatigue pulling him under.

Kelsey's voice woke them hours later, the room now

dim, lit by flickering candles.

"Dinner's ready," she said, setting plates of canned chili and cornbread on the table, a board game already spread out. "Thought we'd have a little send-off for Anna."

Parker grinned, easing into a chair. "A party, huh? Let's do it."

They ate, the chili warm and hearty, their conversation weaving through hopes for the future—self-reliance, rebuilding, maybe even peace. After clearing the plates, they dove into the game Risk. They played until the end, before all getting ready for bed.

The next morning, gunfire cracked in the distance, sharp but not close. Parker jolted awake, his leg throbbing as he reached for his crutches.

Sydney and Kelsey were already in the living room, their faces tense. Anna stood by the door, her backpack slung over her shoulders, the weight of her departure settling over the room.

"Guess this is it," Anna said, adjusting the straps. "Thanks for everything. It's been... well, an adventure."

Parker hobbled over, offering a small smile. "Get home safe. Stay sharp out there."

"Where in Georgia are you headed?" Kelsey asked, her voice soft.

"Trenton," Anna said. "Small town off the highway. Quiet, peaceful. Maybe you guys can visit sometime."

"We'd like that," Sydney said. "Write down your address?"

Anna nodded, taking a notepad from Kelsey and scribbling her details. She handed it back, her eyes lingering on them. "Be safe, okay? Hope to see you in Georgia."

Kelsey pulled her into a hug. "You, too."

Anna stepped out, the door clicking shut behind her. Kelsey turned to Parker and Sydney, her expression wistful. "We'll visit her someday. Feels right."

"Agreed," Parker said, settling onto the couch with his book, though his mind was elsewhere.

They read in silence for a few hours, the morning light filtering through the windows, until the radio crackled. Parker grabbed it, his crutches clattering.

"Parker, what's up?" Leo's voice came through, tinny but clear.

"Been a minute," Parker said. "Just chilling. What's going on?"

"Need help with a project," Leo said. "Building shelves in the basement to move storage down there. My mom's parents showed up—came from central Nashville. Things are getting bad there, so we're setting up a room for them."

Parker glanced at Sydney and Kelsey, who nodded. "We're in," he said. "I'm not much use with the leg, though."

"What happened?" Leo asked.

"I'll explain when we get there," Parker said, switching off the radio. "You guys hear that?"

"Yup," Sydney said, already standing. "Let's get ready."

They dressed quickly—Parker in a fresh flannel, Sydney in jeans and a hoodie—and grabbed their gear, pistols tucked into belts. They walked to Leo's house, the street quiet. Leo answered the door, his eyes widening at Parker's crutches. "Dude, what happened?"

Parker sighed, leaning against the doorframe. He explained what happened while they made their way to the basement to see what the project was.

Leo winced. "That's rough. Glad you're okay, though."

"Thanks," Parker said, glancing at Sydney, who smiled softly.

They followed Leo to the basement, where lanterns cast a warm glow over piles of lumber and tools. "Supplies are here," Leo said. "Just need to build the shelves."

They set to work, measuring and cutting boards, the saw's rasp filling the air. The first shelf was tricky, nails bending until they got the angles right, but the rest went smoother, each one sturdy and level.

Hours later, they hauled the tools back to the garage, sweat beading on their foreheads. Upstairs, Leo's mom had set the dining table with plates of cornbread and beans, steam curling upward.

"Figured you'd be hungry," she said, her smile warm.

"Thanks," Kelsey said, sinking into a chair. "This is great."

"Appreciate the help," Leo said, spooning beans. "Makes room for my grandparents."

"Anytime," Parker said, his leg aching but his spirits high.

They ate in comfortable silence, the food simple but filling. After cleaning up, they chatted briefly, Leo's mom hinting at a "big idea" she wasn't ready to share.

Parker and Sydney left first, Kelsey staying to talk. Back home, Nala greeted them, her tail thumping against the floor.

"How do you think Anna's doing?" Sydney asked, flopping onto the couch.

Parker eased into the armchair, his crutches propped nearby. "Hope she's okay. It's a short trip, but things are dicey out there."

"We should visit her sometime," Sydney said. "Check in."

"Yeah," Parker said, his tone shifting. "But with those warships out there, we've got bigger problems. If they're invading, we need to focus on us—our people."

They tidied the house, dusting shelves and stacking dishes, tasks they'd neglected in the chaos. Kelsey returned, her expression thoughtful.

"What'd you and Leo's mom talk about?" Parker asked.

"Just stuff," Kelsey said, leaning against the counter. "She's got some big plan but wouldn't spill. Could be interesting."

"Hope it's good," Parker said, his mind drifting to the warships, the ring, and the uncertain days ahead...

Chapter 16

Parker Davidson

Parker woke to the faint patter of rain on the roof, the sound pulling him from a restless sleep. His leg ached, a dull throb that hadn't let up since the stabbing. He reached for his crutches, and hobbled to the kitchen, the hardwood cool under his bare feet. The house was quiet, save for Nala's soft snoring in the corner.

He grabbed a water bottle from the counter, its plastic slick with condensation, and took a long sip, the cold soothing his parched throat. They were running low on coffee grounds, and he'd decided to skip his morning cup to stretch their supply.

No stores around here have anything left anyway, he thought, leaning against the counter.

He tested his injured leg, gingerly setting his foot down. A sharp twinge shot through it, not as bad as before but enough to make him wince. He pulled it back, gripping the counter for balance.

Getting there, he told himself, though the slow healing frustrated him.

Sydney shuffled in, her hair mussed, her hoodie

oversized. "Morning," she said, yawning. "You're up early. No coffee?"

"Nah," Parker said, capping the bottle. "Mom said we're down to a few boxes downstairs. Gotta make it last."

Sydney frowned, glancing at the camp stove. "Guess I'll skip it, too. What's on the agenda?"

"Nothing solid," Parker said, easing into a chair at the dining table. "Maybe invite Preston's family over? Haven't seen them in a bit."

"Good idea," Sydney said, grabbing eggs from a basket on the counter, their shells speckled. "Let's check with your mom. Want breakfast?"

"Eggs, right?" Parker asked, a playful edge to his voice.

She grinned, pulling a skillet from the counter. "You know it."

Parker dealt a hand of solitaire as the kitchen filled with the sizzle and savory aroma of scrambled eggs. Nala stirred, her nose twitching, and padded over, hopeful for scraps. Parker scratched her head, her fur warm and soft.

"Want some eggs, girl?" he asked, chuckling.

He finished the game, the cards scattered in a half-solved mess, and stood to grab plates. Forgetting his crutches, he put weight on his bad leg and gasped, pain flaring. He sank back into the chair, cursing under his breath, and reached for the crutches. *Stupid mistake.*

In the kitchen, he grabbed two plates, and set them on the table. Sydney slid the eggs onto them, golden and steaming, and they ate in comfortable silence, dropping a few scraps for Nala, who gobbled them eagerly. *Eggs every morning's getting old, but it's what we've got.*

He opened the back door to let Nala out, the air heavy with the scent of impending rain. Dark clouds loomed overhead, promising a downpour. *Good. We need the water.*

Kelsey came downstairs, her sweater loose, her hair still damp from the previous day's shower.

"Any eggs left?" she asked, peering at the skillet.

"A bit," Sydney said, scraping the last of the eggs onto a plate. "Want me to make more?"

"Nah, this'll do," Kelsey said, sitting down. "Thanks."

A knock at the door broke the quiet, and Nala barked, scrambling back inside. Parker hobbled over, opening it to find Preston, his flannel damp from the morning's humidity.

"Hey," Preston said. "You got those big rain barrels outside? Saw the clouds—figured you'd want to catch the water."

"Good call," Parker said. "The others are in the garage. Could you help move them?"

"Yep," Preston said, stepping inside. "Gotta tweak the gutters, though. They're too long—water'll miss the barrels."

"Didn't know they came apart," Parker said, leading him through the house.

"Easy fix," Preston said. "Just unscrew the lower segments."

In the garage, the air smelled of sawdust and motor oil. Parker pointed to the blue plastic barrels stacked against the wall. Preston hauled the first one outside, positioning it under a gutter by the back door. He climbed a stepladder, unscrewing the lower gutter segment with a quick twist, tossing it into the grass. "Keep this?" he asked.

"Might as well," Parker said, leaning on his crutches. "Could come in handy."

Preston set up the second barrel, repeating the process, the metal gutter piece clattering as it hit the ground. The barrels stood ready, their open tops poised to catch the rain. "Hope it pours," Parker said, glancing at the sky. "We're low on water."

"Fingers crossed," Preston said, wiping his hands on his jeans. "Anything else you need?"

"No, I think we're good for now," Parker said. "Thanks, though."

"No problem," Preston said, heading out. "Angelina and Bella are making pancakes. Gotta get back."

"Pancakes?" Parker said, his mouth watering. "Might have some mix in the basement. Eggs are getting old fast."

Preston laughed. "Tell me about it."

He waved and left, the front door clicking shut behind him.

~

Leo Boone

Leo woke to the soft glow of sunrise filtering through his bedroom window, the sky streaked with gray clouds promising rain. He pulled on a faded T-shirt and jeans, the fabric cool against his skin, and glanced down the hall. His mom's door was shut, as was his grandparents', their snores a faint hum through the walls.

He padded downstairs, the house quiet except for the creak of the stairs, and set up the camp stove in the kitchen. The air filled with the rich, bitter scent of coffee as he boiled water, pouring it into a mug with powdered creamer that clumped slightly as he stirred.

He carried the mug to the front porch, settling into a wicker chair that groaned under his weight. The street was still, the air heavy with the threat of rain, and he sipped the coffee, its warmth spreading through him as he watched the empty road. The neighborhood felt smaller now, the world shrinking under the weight of the EMP's aftermath.

His thoughts drifted to his neighbors, Mr. and Mrs. Frank, the elderly couple next door. They'd always been self-sufficient, their garden thriving even before the power went out, but he hadn't checked on them since the chaos began. *Today's as good a day as any*, he thought, finishing his coffee.

He returned inside and rinsed his coffee mug, setting it on the towel to dry. He slipped his shoes on and made his way over to the neighbors house. He was never close with them, but had helped them out when they needed it.

Leo knocked lightly on the door, a moment later Mrs. Frank slowly opened the door just enough to see him. "Can I help you?"

"I just wanted to come see how you guys are doing."

"We're doing fine, thank you," she said, shutting the door, the deadbolt audibly being opened.

They must be trying to keep to themselves. I'll respect that, if I had it my way I would too.

Back home, his mom was in the kitchen, stirring oatmeal on the camp stove, the sweet smell mingling with the lingering coffee aroma.

"Where were you?" she asked, glancing over her shoulder.

"Checking on the Franks," Leo said, setting his mug in the sink. "They say they're fine, but Mrs. Frank seemed jumpy."

His mom frowned, spoon pausing mid-stir. "They've always been stubborn. Probably just shaken up by everything. Did they need anything?"

"Nope," Leo said, sitting at the table. "Said they're good, but I'll keep an eye out."

"Good idea," she said, ladling oatmeal into bowls. "Things are only getting tougher out there."

Leo nodded, his thoughts drifting to the warships Parker had mentioned, the uncertainty of what lay ahead. The rain began to fall, a soft patter against the windows, and he hoped it would bring some relief to their dwindling water supply

Chapter 17
Parker Davidson

Parker jolted awake from a nap, his leg throbbing as he shifted on the couch. The house was eerily quiet, but shouts pierced the air from outside, sharp and urgent. He reached for his crutches, then hesitated, testing his injured leg. He stood, wincing as a dull ache pulsed through it, but kept going, driven by the commotion. In the kitchen, he grabbed his pistol from the counter, its grip cool and familiar, and hobbled to the front door, Nala trailing behind, her ears perked.

"What's going on out here?" he called, stepping onto the porch. The air was heavy with the scent of rain-soaked grass. Across the street, Preston stood in his driveway, his stance tense. In their own driveway, Kelsey and Sydney faced three figures in the road—Parker's old classmate, Alex, and two rough-looking guys, their jackets patched and dirty. Alex's eyes locked on Parker, a smirk twisting his lips.

"Why are you here, Alex?" Sydney shouted, her voice sharp. "We're not helping you, and you know it."

"Wanna bet?" Alex shot back, his tone mocking. "Get

him, boys."

The two men charged toward Preston, their boots pounding the pavement. Alex raised a pistol, aiming it at Kelsey, Sydney, and Parker. Across the street, Preston grunted as the men tackled him, fists and kicks flying in a brutal blur.

Kelsey screamed, her voice raw, "Stop it! Get off him!"

Parker's grip tightened on his pistol, but with Preston in the fray, he couldn't risk a shot. He stumbled toward Sydney and Kelsey, his leg protesting with every step.

"Parker," Alex sneered, his gun steady. "Been looking for you."

"What for—" A gunshot cut Parker off, echoing through the neighborhood.

Everyone froze, eyes darting to Preston. One of Alex's men lay crumpled on the ground, blood pooling beneath him. Preston staggered to his feet, clutching a pistol, his face bloodied but fierce. He aimed at the second man, who raised his hands in surrender. Another shot rang out, and the man collapsed, lifeless.

Preston turned his gun on Alex, his voice a low growl. "Drop it, or you're next."

Alex hesitated, his smirk fading, then lowered his pistol, letting it clatter to the pavement. Preston advanced, his face a mask of fury, and leaned in close, whispering something Parker couldn't hear.

Alex's eyes widened, and he bolted down the street, his footsteps fading into the distance. Preston picked up the fallen pistol and crossed to Parker's group, his breath ragged, blood streaking his cheek.

Kelsey took the pistol, tucking it into her waistband. "We need to get you to Chris," she said, her voice steady despite the chaos. "You took a hell of a beating."

Kelsey and Preston headed across the street to Chris's clinic, while Parker and Sydney returned inside, Nala nudging Parker's hand as they settled in the living room. Sydney sank onto the couch, her face pale.

"What did Alex want?" he asked.

"He was looking for you. He didn't say what for, but he was serious." Sydney asked, "How do you know him?"

Parker leaned back, his leg propped on a stool. "We were friends in sophomore year, but he got into some bad stuff—started a gang. They were behind most of the crime around here before the EMP. Now? I think they're just stirring up trouble for the hell of it."

Sydney's eyes narrowed. "A gang? So they're just... what, roaming around causing problems?"

"Pretty much," Parker said. "Alex has always been a troublemaker. He's got a crew now, and they're not stopping anytime soon."

"We need to be on high alert," Sydney said, her fingers twisting the ring on her finger, a nervous habit since the proposal. "If they're targeting you, we can't let our guard down."

Parker nodded. "I want to warn Leo and Preston. The police won't be much help—they've been after Alex's crew for years. Found their hideout once, but two officers died, and they never tried again."

Sydney frowned. "They're trained for this. Why can't they handle it?"

"They're outmatched," Parker said, sipping water from a bottle. "Alex's group is slippery. Always has been. A rag-tag team of teenagers out to make a quick buck."

They crossed the street to Preston's house, finding Leo there, his eyes wide as he saw Parker walking without crutches.

"Dude, you're mobile already?" he asked.

"Barely," Parker said, grimacing. "Hurts like hell, but I'm pushing through."

"Careful," Chris called from the kitchen, where he was cleaning Preston's cuts, the sharp scent of antiseptic in the air.

"I'm fine," Parker said, waving him off. "But I need to tell you guys something. Alex, the kid who started this? He runs a gang. They were trouble before the EMP—most of the crime in our area was them. Now they're just causing chaos. Sydney said they were looking for me, so they're probably not done."

Preston winced as Chris taped gauze to his forehead. "Great. We need to watch our backs."

"What can we do?" Chris asked, his hands steady as he worked. "If they're a big group, we're outnumbered."

"We prep," Parker said, his voice firm. "Get ready for a fight. They're after me, so they'll keep coming. We can't just sit here."

"Prepping takes time," Chris said, frowning. "And we can't afford to tangle with every random group out there."

"Agreed," Parker said. "We focus on our people—our supplies, our safety. No outsiders unless they're useful or have intel."

Chris nodded, then shifted topics. "Speaking of intel, those warships on the coast—any updates?"

Kelsey, leaning against the counter, spoke up. "When Anna and I were traveling, we heard the ships were moving closer. I think they pulled back to shield from the EMP, but now they're staging for a ground invasion."

"How long do we have?" Chris asked, wrapping more gauze.

"Depends on the coastal states' resistance," Kelsey said. "Could be days, could be a month."

"If they break through, they'll be weaker," Preston said, his voice hoarse. "But we still need to be ready."

Angelina stepped into the room, balancing an armful of water bottles.

"What about the gun store in town?" she said. "If we clear it out, we control the weapons. Keeps them out of that gang's hands and gives us an edge against invaders."

Parker's eyes lit up, then dimmed. "Problem is, we killed the owner and his friend last time we was there. Cops might've locked it down."

"Worth checking," Preston said. "If it's open, we grab everything—guns, ammo, all of it. Tonight, before sunrise. Fewer people awake."

"Agreed," Parker said. "We all go. Preston, Chris, Leo, take your truck. Mom, Sydney, and I will take ours. We move fast, load up, and get out."

"See you before dark," Leo said, heading out.

Parker, Sydney, and Kelsey returned home, the air heavy with the day's events. "Pack your bags," Sydney said, shutting the door. "We need to be ready."

As the sky darkened, Parker checked his backpack—flashlight, extra magazines, a knife. His leg ached, but he ignored it, focusing on the task. He clicked the radio. "Leo, Preston, Chris, let's roll."

"Copy," they replied.

Parker, Sydney, and Kelsey piled into their truck, the engine rumbling to life. Across the street, Preston's truck idled. They drove to the gun store, the streets empty, the air thick with the scent of rain. Pulling into the lot, they saw no one—no cops, no looters.

Lucky break, Parker thought.

They backed the trucks to the door for quick loading.

Leo tugged the handle, and it opened with a creak. "Unlocked," he said. "Cops never came."

Inside, the store smelled of dust and metal, untouched since Parker's last visit. He limped to the back, stacking rifles on the counter—AR-15s, shotguns, a few hunting rifles. The others ferried them to the trucks, their footsteps echoing. Parker checked the back for pistols but found only three, their grips worn.

Most of the handguns are up front. Moving to the showcase shelf, its glass smudged but intact, he grabbed every pistol, setting them on the counter as Sydney and Kelsey loaded them into the truck.

"Bed's full," Preston said, poking his head in. "Any more guns?"

"Just ammo now," Parker said. "Big boxes in the back—thousand rounds each. Heavy."

Preston and Leo joined him, hauling crates of *9mm*, *.45*, and *.223* ammo, their arms straining. The sun's first rays peeked over the horizon as they cleared the last box. "Time to go," Chris said, wiping sweat from his brow.

They loaded into the trucks, the beds sagging with their haul, and sped back, pulling into their driveways as the neighborhood stirred. Parker opened the garage, and they unloaded frantically, stacking guns and ammo against the walls.

"We'll sort them later," Kelsey said, her voice urgent. "Sun's up—people will notice."

"Agreed," Parker said, shutting the garage door. Inside, they collapsed into the living room, Nala circling excitedly. Parker scooped kibble into her bowl, her tail thumping as she ate.

"That went better than expected," Kelsey said, setting out plates for breakfast. "We've got the firepower now."

"Yeah," Sydney said, pulling eggs from the basket. "But if Alex's gang was after the same thing, they'll be pissed."

Parker nodded, his mind racing. "They'd need weapons to arm recruits. But why so many? Who are they fighting? Two guns pointed at them, and most people would back off."

"We'll have to find out," Sydney said, cracking eggs into the skillet, the sizzle filling the kitchen.

They ate breakfast, the eggs warm but repetitive, and discussed Alex's gang. "We need eyes on them," Parker said. "Figure out their next move."

After eating, they split up to clean the house, dusting shelves and sweeping floors. A knock at the door interrupted them. Parker answered, finding Preston.

"Got visitors," he said. "Couple with a kid from North Carolina. Say it's urgent."

"I'll come," Parker said, grabbing his pistol, his leg aching but steady.

Across the street, the couple sat on Preston's back porch, their faces drawn, a young girl clinging to her mother's side.

"You're from North Carolina?" Parker asked, standing with Preston.

The man nodded, his voice hoarse. "Had to flee. Ground invasion hit the coast."

Parker's blood ran cold. He glanced at Preston, who looked equally grim. "How big?"

"Not huge," the man said, his eyes distant. "No tanks, just infantry. But they're organized. Most folks didn't fight back—just a few families, including ours." His voice broke, his wife sobbing quietly. "We lost our oldest son. He went with neighbors to fight. Never came back."

"I'm so sorry," Parker said, his chest tightening. "Preston, we need to act. If the coast's falling, they could hit Nashville any day."

"We should talk to the mayor," Preston said. "Government's gotta have faraday-caged radios. They could alert the military, get word to the president."

"We have to try," Parker said. "Otherwise, we're sitting ducks."

The couple nodded, their daughter's eyes wide with fear. Parker's mind raced—Alex's gang, the invasion, the guns in the garage. The world was closing in, and they had to be ready.

Chapter 18
Parker Davidson

Parker watched Preston sling a backpack over his shoulder, the fabric straining with the weight of supplies. The air in the Sanchez living room was thick with tension, the North Carolina family's story of invasion still echoing in their minds. Preston grabbed his truck keys from the counter, the metal jangling.

"Go get them," he said, his voice low but firm.

Parker nodded, limping to the backyard where the family sat on weathered patio chairs, the young girl clutching her mother's hand. The air smelled of damp grass and the faint tang of smoke from a distant fire.

"Hey," Parker called. "We need you to come with us to the mayor."

The family stood, their faces drawn but resolute, and followed Parker through the house to the driveway. Preston's truck idled, its engine a low rumble, exhaust curling in the morning air. They piled in—Parker, the family, and Preston—cramming into the bench seats, the girl wedged between her parents.

The drive to the city's main shopping district was

quiet, the streets littered with abandoned cars and debris. They pulled up to City Hall, a squat brick building with boarded windows, and Preston parked in the empty lot, gravel crunching under the tires.

As they approached the entrance, a burly officer in a faded uniform stepped forward, his hand raised.

"You can't go in without an invitation," he said, his voice gruff.

Preston pushed past, his jaw set. "We need to see the mayor. Now."

Parker and the family followed, the officer's protests fading as they climbed the central staircase, its marble steps chipped and dusty. They reached the mayor's office, heavy oak door ajar, and stepped inside. The mayor, a wiry man with glasses perched on his nose, sat at a desk, typing on a solar-powered laptop—an unexpected sight in the post-EMP world.

"Mr. Mayor," Preston said, his voice cutting through the hum of the laptop's fan. "We need to talk."

Two officers burst in, grabbing Preston's arms.

"Out, now," one barked.

"Stop," the mayor said, raising a hand. "Let them speak." The officers released Preston, retreating with sour looks.

Preston straightened, brushing off his jacket. "This family came to my house from North Carolina. They say a foreign military's invaded the coast. You've got comms with the governor, right?"

The mayor nodded, his eyes narrowing. "What's it to you?"

"This is serious," Parker interjected. "They've got

details—cities, numbers. You need to hear it."

The mayor gestured to the family. "Tell me everything. City, scale, anything relevant. I'll send it to the governor."

The man cleared his throat, his voice hoarse. "We're from Wilmington. Ground forces hit the coast—no vehicles, just infantry. Hundreds, maybe thousands. Organized, with rifles and body armor. Most folks fled; some fought but didn't last long." His wife's eyes welled up, her hand tightening on their daughter's. "We lost our son trying to hold them off."

The mayor's fingers flew across the keyboard, recording every detail. When the man finished, the mayor hit a key, likely sending the message.

"Thank you," he said, his tone grave. "The governor will pass this to the president. He probably knows, but this confirms it. He can activate military units to defend the coasts."

"We'll bring any more intel we get," Preston said, his voice steady.

The mayor nodded, already turning back to his screen. They left the office, descending the stairs in silence, the weight of the invasion settling over them. Back in the truck, Preston glanced at the family in the rearview mirror.

"You can stay with us a couple days, but you'll need to find somewhere else after that."

"Thank you," the man said, his voice breaking. "We're grateful."

They returned to Preston's house, the truck's shocks creaking as they parked. Parker crossed the street to his own home, his leg aching but manageable without crutches.

Inside, he found Kelsey at the dining table, a mug of weak tea in her hands, the air smelling faintly of chamomile.

"Where's Sydney?" he asked.

"Napping," Kelsey said, setting the mug down. "She was wiped out."

Parker nodded, easing into a chair. "Preston needed me. That family from North Carolina—they confirmed the invasion. Foreign troops hit the coast. We took them to the mayor; he's got a computer, comms with the governor."

Kelsey's eyes widened. "So it's real? The warships?"

"Yeah," Parker said, his stomach twisting. "They could reach Nashville in a week, maybe two. We need to be ready for anything."

Kelsey leaned back, her expression grim. "That's life now, isn't it? Always ready, never stopping."

Parker nodded, then headed to the backyard to feed the chickens. The air was cool, the sky overcast, promising more rain. He scattered feed, the hens clucking eagerly, and collected their eggs, their shells warm in his hands. Back inside, he set the eggs on the counter and joined Kelsey in the dining room, his mind heavy with the day's revelations.

~

Preston Sanchez

Preston led the North Carolina family to the guest

room, where Angelina was already spreading fresh sheets across the bed, the fabric snapping as she tucked it in.

"You can settle here," he said. "Help us clean the house, and we'll figure out food and water."

The man nodded, his wife offering a tired smile as their daughter clutched a stuffed bear.

Preston headed downstairs, where Chris was knee-deep in the fridge, tossing out spoiled food—moldy cheese, rancid milk, the stench sharp and sour.

"Should've done this days ago," Chris muttered, tossing a container into a trash bag.

Preston opened the windows, letting the breeze sweep away the smell, the curtains fluttering. Bella bounded downstairs, her pigtails bouncing, clutching a coloring book and a pack of crayons.

"Can I draw, Daddy?" she asked, her voice bright.

"Sure, kiddo," Preston said, setting her up at the dining table, the wood scarred from years of use. He and Chris hauled the trash bags outside, the weight pulling at their arms, and dumped them in a bin by the garage. Back inside, they swept the kitchen floor, the broom's bristles scraping against linoleum, and wiped down counters until they gleamed.

With the kitchen done, Preston sat with Bella, coloring a picture of a horse, the crayons' waxy scent nostalgic. She giggled as he shaded the mane bright blue. When she grew bored, he helped her gather her supplies and sent her upstairs, her footsteps pattering.

"Dinner soon?" Angelina called from the kitchen, where pots clattered on the camp stove.

"Yeah," Preston said. "Double the usual—they're probably starving after their trip."

Angelina nodded, stirring a pot of beans and rice, the savory aroma filling the house. Preston checked on Bella, finding her asleep on her bed, her coloring book open beside her. He draped a blanket over her, its edges frayed, and closed the door softly. Downstairs, the family waited at the dining table, the girl's eyes heavy but curious. Angelina set the pot on the table, steam curling upward, and they ate, the family sharing stories of their escape—narrow misses, abandoned homes, the grief of their lost son.

After dinner, the family retired to the guest room, their footsteps heavy on the stairs. Preston helped Angelina clean, scrubbing dishes in a bucket of rainwater, the water sloshing. They finished and headed to bed, the house quiet except for the faint creak of settling wood.

The next morning, Preston woke to the cool touch of dawn, the air crisp as he stepped into the backyard. He breathed deeply, the grass damp under his boots, then returned inside for a water bottle. In the garage, he surveyed the guns and ammo from the raid, their metal glinting in the dim light. He opened the garage door, letting sunlight spill in, and grabbed a notebook to inventory the haul—boxes of *9mm, .45, .223,* and shotgun shells, rifles stacked haphazardly.

Across the street, Parker was doing the same, his silhouette visible in his garage. Preston waved, then continued sorting, stacking ammo boxes on a shelf, their labels faded but legible. The shelf groaned under the weight, nearly full. The guns were trickier—no room to organize properly, so he piled them neatly in a corner. When he finished, he crossed to Parker's, his boots crunching on the driveway.

"Morning," he called. "How's your haul?"

"Pretty good," Parker said, flipping through a notebook. "Mostly ARs, some pistols. You?"

"Couple thousand rounds per caliber, a few hundred for shotguns," Preston said. "Mostly rifles, some shotguns. Wanna trade to even things out?"

"Yeah," Parker said. "Gives us both a solid mix. Help me with the ammo first?"

Preston nodded, grabbing boxes of ammo, reading labels—*9mm, .308*—and stacking them by the door. They worked quickly. When they finished, Parker tossed the notebook onto the pile and limped to the backyard, checking the rain barrels.

"Full enough for showers," he said, grinning. "You, Angelina, and Bella want a turn?"

"Please," Preston said, his skin itching from days without a proper wash. "We'll bring clothes."

"Anytime," Parker said. "Just don't use too much water."

~

Parker Davidson

Preston jogged across the street, and Parker entered the house, finding Kelsey awake, sipping tea at the dining table.

"Morning," he said. "Been sorting the guns and

ammo."

"What'd we get?" she asked, setting her mug down.

Parker grabbed the notebook from the garage, its pages scrawled with counts—twelve ARs, eight pistols, thousands of rounds. He handed it to her, watching her eyes widen.

"More than I thought," she said.

"Yeah," Parker said. "Preston's got more rifles and shotguns. We'll trade later for a balanced arsenal. They're coming over to shower soon."

"Good," Kelsey said. "We should figure out laundry, too. Clean clothes would be nice."

"Thought about that," Parker said. "We've got an empty barrel. Cut it in half, use each as a washtub. Soak clothes with detergent, then hang them on a clothesline."

Kelsey nodded. "We've got one empty, right? Plus the fuel and water barrels?"

"Yup," Parker said. "Let's do it now."

In the garage, Parker grabbed the empty barrel and a handsaw from the toolbox, its handle worn smooth. Kelsey steadied the barrel as he sawed, the blade rasping through plastic, splitting it into two uneven halves. They carried them to the backyard, propping them against the house. Preston approached with Angelina and Bella, clean clothes draped over their arms.

"Give us a sec," Parker said, grabbing the hose from the shower setup. He filled the barrel halves, water glugging softly, and returned the hose.

"Laundry tubs," he explained. "Figured clean clothes are overdue."

"Smart," Preston said. "Thanks for the showers. We'll be quick."

"No rush," Parker said, waving them off. "Just don't drain us dry."

Kelsey emerged with a laundry basket and a bottle of detergent, the cap sticky with residue. She dumped clothes into one tub, pouring in detergent, the scent sharp and clean. Once they were done in the detergent tub she threw it all into the other with water to rinse. Parker grabbed his own basket, mimicking her. They strung paracord from the garage to the fence, nailing it taut, and wrung out their clothes, draping them over the line. The wastewater was poured into a corner of the yard, dubbed the "dump zone".

Parker went inside to wake Sydney.

"Hey, grab your laundry," he called. "We've got tubs set up."

Sydney appeared, bleary-eyed, a basket of clothes in tow. Parker showed her the process, and she took over, scrubbing her jeans with focus. He sank onto the couch, satisfied with what he'd gotten done, though his leg was aching. But clean clothes, full barrels, a stocked arsenal—the world was falling apart, but they were holding their own.

Chapter 19
Mary Southerland

Mary Southerland trudged along the cracked highway on-ramp, her boots scuffing against the asphalt, each step a battle against the ache in her blistered feet. She'd been walking for over two weeks, covering nearly twenty-five hundred miles from Everett, Washington, where she'd been working with Kelsey Davidson when the EMP hit. The journey had been brutal—days of endless roads, nights under stars or in strangers' barns, sustained by the kindness of passersby who offered rides, food, or a moment's rest. Her backpack, now frayed and caked with dust, weighed heavy on her shoulders, but the sight of the Nashville neighborhood in the distance sparked a flicker of hope.

Almost there, she thought, her heart pounding with anticipation and exhaustion.

Mary and Kelsey weren't close, but they'd shared enough coffee breaks and late-night shifts to form a bond. When Kelsey had left Everett almost immediately to return to her son Parker, Mary knew she had to do the same for her daughter, Sydney. She'd hoped to cross paths with Kelsey on the road, maybe share a ride in a rare working vehicle, but their paths never converged.

She must've gotten lucky with a car, Mary mused, her breath shallow as she pushed forward.

The thought of Sydney, alone and worried, gnawed at her. She trusted Parker—had known him since he was a lanky teenager, before he and Sydney started dating. He was steady, resourceful, the kind of person who'd keep her daughter safe in this chaotic new world.

The neighborhood's main street came into view, modest houses lining the road, their yards overgrown but quiet. Mary's memory of Parker's address was hazy, but she recalled it was on this street.

Her legs trembled, each step a chore, her feet screaming with every movement. The sidewalk stretched endlessly, the heat shimmering off the pavement, mingling with the faint smell of rain-soaked earth from the previous day's storm. Up ahead, three figures, all seeming to be in a hurry, crossed the street—two kept walking, but one stopped, turning toward her.

The man approached, his flannel shirt patched at the elbows, his eyes cautious.

"Who are you?" he asked, his hand resting near his belt where a knife glinted.

Mary cleared her throat, the dryness catching her words. "I'm looking for Parker Davidson's house."

He studied her, then pointed to a house two doors down, its porch sagging but sturdy. "That one. Why?"

"I need to see him," she said, too tired to explain. "Thanks."

She shuffled forward, her vision blurring as she neared the house. Twice her knees buckled, but she caught herself, gripping a mailbox for support.

At the front door, she knocked, the sound weak against the wood. No answer. She knocked again, harder, her knuckles aching. The door creaked open, and Parker stood there, his face etched with concern; Nala barked behind him, her tail thumping.

"Can I help you?" he asked, then froze. "Mary? You made it!"

She managed a weak smile, her voice raspy. "Long trip."

Parker turned, shouting into the house. "Sydney, get out here!"

Footsteps thundered, and Sydney appeared, her eyes widening.

"Mom!" She rushed forward, enveloping Mary in a hug, tears streaming down her face. "I thought... I was so worried."

Mary clung to her, the warmth of her daughter's embrace melting the weeks of fear and fatigue.

"I'm here now," she whispered, her voice breaking.

"Let's get you cleaned up," Sydney said, guiding her inside. "Food, water, a shower—you need it all."

Sydney led her to the backyard, showing her to the shower and leaving her to use it.

Mary stepped in, shrieking as the cold water hit her skin, washing away layers of grime and sweat. The chill was a shock and a relief, cleansing the road's toll from her body. She dried off with a rough towel, slipped into clean clothes from her pack, and felt human again. Inside, a bowl of vegetable soup steamed on the dining table, a water bottle beside it, the condensation cool against her palm.

"If you need more, just say," Parker called from the kitchen, his voice warm.

Mary nodded, settling into a chair, the wood creaking. The soup's warmth soothed her raw throat, each spoonful a small comfort after weeks of scavenging.

Sydney sat across from her, her eyes bright with relief. "Tell me everything," she said, leaning forward.

Mary recounted her journey—hitchhiking with other travelers, sleeping in abandoned gas stations, trading work for food. Between sips of water, she described the kindness of strangers and the terror of dodging looters.

Sydney listened, her face a mix of awe and worry, then shared her own story: the EMP, staying with Parker, the gang trouble, and, with a shy smile, her engagement.

Mary's heart swelled, glancing at the ring glinting on Sydney's finger.

After finishing, Mary cleaned her bowl, setting it to dry on a towel. In the living room, she sank onto the couch, its cushions soft but worn.

"So you've been here since the EMP?" she asked Sydney.

"Yeah," Sydney said, sitting beside her. "Safer here with Parker and Kelsey. Better than being alone."

"Smart," Mary said, her eyelids heavy. "I need to lie down. My feet are killing me—blisters on blisters."

Sydney led her upstairs to a guest room, where Kelsey and Parker had made up a bed, the sheets crisp despite the circumstances. Mary dropped her backpack by the door and collapsed onto the mattress, the softness a luxury after weeks on hard ground. She was asleep before her head hit the pillow.

~

Parker Davidson

Parker descended the stairs, finding Sydney on the couch, her book open but unread, her eyes distant with relief.

"Happy your mom's home?" he asked, settling beside her.

"Ecstatic," Sydney said, her voice soft. "I was starting to think she'd never make it."

"Me too," Parker said, pulling her into a hug, her warmth grounding him. "I'm just glad she's safe."

They read in silence, Parker flipping through one of Kelsey's survival manuals—tips on water purification, shelter-building, skills that felt vital now. The pages were worn, the ink smudged from years of use. He glanced up as Kelsey approached, holding the radio, her expression tense.

"Preston's in town," she said. "Saw Alex again."

Parker and Sydney snapped to attention. "What?" they said in unison.

"He's not causing trouble—yet," Kelsey said. "But he's there, with his crew."

Parker's stomach tightened. "Should we check it out?"

Kelsey hesitated, her fingers tapping the radio. "Maybe, but we can't be seen. Too risky."

"Preston shouldn't be alone," Parker said, standing,

his leg aching but manageable. "I'm going."

"I'm in too," Kelsey said, her jaw set. "But we stay low."

"Grab the new ARs," Parker said, heading to the garage. He selected two rifles, their metal cool and heavy, and loaded magazines with a satisfying click. Back inside, he handed one to Kelsey, who checked it with practiced ease.

"Be careful," Sydney called from the couch, her voice soft but teasing. "No more stabbings."

Parker chuckled, despite the tension. "I'll try."

They left, locking the door, and moved swiftly through the neighborhood, the air thick with the scent of wet pavement.

At the shopping district, they found Preston crouched behind a rusted sedan in the pawn shop's lot, his eyes fixed on the grocery store across the street. "Alex is there," he whispered. "Three guys with him."

Parker and Kelsey joined him, peering over the car's hood. Alex stood by the store's entrance, gesturing animatedly to his crew, their jackets patched and worn. They pushed a cart inside, emerging minutes later with it piled high—canned goods, batteries, a few tools glinting in the sunlight.

"Resupply run?" Preston murmured.

"Looks like it," Parker said, his eyes narrowing. "Question is, did they pay or just take it?"

"Don't want to get close enough to find out," Kelsey said, her voice low.

"Let's move," Preston said. "They might hit another store."

They slipped along the storefronts, staying low, and crossed to the neighborhood, their steps quick but silent.

At the split to their houses, Parker turned to Preston. "Keep us posted if anything else happens."

Preston nodded, heading up his driveway. Parker and Kelsey entered their house, locking the door. Sydney looked up from her book. "What happened?"

"We watched Alex and his guys hit the grocery store," Parker said, unloading his AR and setting it on the counter. "Got a cart full of stuff. Don't know if they paid or strong-armed it. We left before they saw us."

Sydney frowned. "He's planning something. I can feel it."

Parker sank onto the couch, his leg throbbing. "What if we got someone to spy on them? Figure out their size, their plans. Maybe take them down."

Kelsey nodded, leaning against the wall. "Smart, but it'd need to be someone we trust. Someone willing to risk it, who knows what to look for."

"And someone Alex doesn't know," Parker added. "If he recognizes them, it's over."

"What about Sam?" Sydney said, her eyes lighting up. "Your high school friend. You trust him, and he never ran with Alex's crowd."

Parker snapped his fingers. "Perfect. But we need to find him first."

"We'll work on that," Sydney said. "But we need a solid plan—escape routes, backups, like a real operation. Anything could go wrong."

"The sooner, the better," Kelsey said. "Before Alex's gang makes their move."

Parker nodded, his mind racing. He headed to his bedroom, the weight of the day settling in. Lying on his bed, he thought about the church—could the pastor still marry them?—and the spy plan. Sam was the right call, but where was he? The invasion loomed, Alex's gang was a growing threat, and time was slipping away. He closed his eyes, trying to prioritize, but exhaustion pulled him under, and he drifted into a restless sleep.

Chapter 20

Alex Carpenter

Alex stood in the grocery store's parking lot, the air heavy with the scent of asphalt and distant rain. His crew—Hector, Michael, and Jack—unloaded the cart, piling canned goods, batteries, and tools into the trunk of their battered sedan. The haul clinked and rattled, a small fortune in a world where cash was losing value.

Hector opened the back door with a creak, and Alex slid in, the worn leather seat cool against his jeans. Hector followed, slamming the door, while Michael took the driver's seat, and Jack hopped in beside him. The engine sputtered to life, and they pulled out, the tires crunching gravel as they headed for their hideout.

Alex had built his gang from nothing in high school, with Hector, Michael, and Jack as his first recruits. They'd stuck by him through every scheme, their loyalty forged in late-night heists and narrow escapes.

When they'd bought the old warehouse on Nashville's outskirts, the seller—a grizzled man eager to offload the property—had raised an eyebrow at their intentions but took the cash without questions.

The warehouse, nestled in a shallow valley between rolling hills, was perfect: accessible only by a rutted dirt road that deterred outsiders. Inside, they'd transformed it, partitioning it with shelves for their black-market goods—stolen luxury items, high-end electronics, even the occasional exotic pet swiped from a wealthy home. The thrill of the game, the rush of dodging the law, kept Alex hooked, even if he sometimes questioned the life he'd chosen.

Recently, he'd escalated to store robberies, assembling a dedicated crew for these high-stakes jobs. They struck under cover of night, every couple of weeks, moving fast to avoid trouble. Alex rarely joined them, preferring to manage sales from the warehouse, but the botched encounter with Parker Davidson had shaken him.

Peter and Xavier, two of his oldest members, had died trying to strong-arm Parker into joining. Alex had wanted Parker since the gang's early days—his resourcefulness would've been an asset—but Parker's refusal, coupled with his defiance, had made him a target. Now, with Hector and Jack as his bodyguards, Alex never moved alone.

Michael pulled into the warehouse's back lot, the car bouncing over potholes. Hector hopped out, holding the door for Alex, who gritted his teeth at the gesture.

"I can open my own door," he muttered, but Hector insisted, his eyes scanning the shadows. Inside, a group of younger members scrambled to unload the car, stacking goods on the incoming shelves. The warehouse smelled of dust and oil, its concrete floor stained from years of neglect. Alex paced the aisles, eyeing their inventory—designer watches, gold chains, rare liquors.

Once cash is worthless, this'll be gold, he thought.

"We could trade these for anything," he said to Hector. "Luxury items, no power needed. People will want them."

Hector shrugged, kicking a crate. "Maybe. Depends if they care about this junk when they're starving."

"Then we keep robbing," Alex said, his voice sharp. "More goods, more power."

Jack approached, wiping sweat from his brow. "Want me to get the boys for another run?"

"Do it," Alex said. "I'll work out a plan."

Jack jogged to the break room, a corner of the warehouse with mismatched chairs and a battered coffee maker. Most of the gang lounged there between jobs, swapping stories or playing cards. Alex continued his rounds, picking up a silver cigarette case, its weight satisfying in his hand. *This'll trade well*, he thought, setting it down.

"Alex!" Jack called from the break room. "Need you!"

Alex crossed the warehouse, the echo of his boots sharp against the concrete. The crew sat around a folding table, their faces expectant.

"Listen up," Alex said, leaning forward. "Cash is dying. Our luxury goods—watches, jewelry, booze—will run the market soon. We've got a solid start, but we need more. Bigger hauls, bigger groups for safety. Same playbook, bolder heists."

The room buzzed with agreement, murmurs rippling through the group.

"We'll hit more stores," Alex continued. "Maybe houses, too. Control the supply, we control the trade."

They nodded, dispersing to prepare, and Alex retreated to his office, a cramped room with a desk and a flickering lantern. He sank into his chair, the wood creaking, and scribbled a list—jewelry, alcohol, tobacco.

Tobacco's a goldmine, he realized.

"Jack!" he shouted.

Jack burst in, breathless. "Boss?"

"Tell everyone to grab tobacco products; they're a goldmine."

Jack nodded and left, closing the door. Alex jotted more notes, then headed to the break room for coffee, the bitter aroma grounding him. As night fell, he grew restless, pacing the warehouse, awaiting the first haul.

When a car rolled in, he opened a garage door, its rusted hinges groaning. The crew unloaded crates of liquor, clothing, and electronics, piling them on the shelves. Alex cataloged each item in his notebook, his pen scratching as Jack and Hector sorted. The night stretched on, car after car, until sunrise painted the sky orange. They'd scored hundreds of items—enough to dominate any trade.

But a worry nagged him. The police were still active, and trading luxury goods openly would draw attention.

Teenagers with thousands in stolen goods? They'll know it's us.

He returned to his office, exhaustion pulling at him, and closed his eyes, intending a brief rest. Hours later, Jack's voice jolted him awake.

"Alex!"

"What?" Alex snapped, rubbing his face. "I was sleeping."

"The guys want to know about another raid," Jack said, leaning in the doorway.

Alex shrugged, his mind foggy. "Maybe. I need coffee first."

"I'm brewing a pot," Jack said, disappearing.

Alex grabbed his pen, clicking it absently, and sipped the coffee Jack brought, its heat burning his throat.

"Today's plan?" Jack asked.

"Recruitment," Alex said. "We need more bodies. The cops will come for us once we start trading. How many to take them down?"

Jack hesitated. "Six, seven?"

"Then get me seven," Alex said. "And shut the door."

Jack left, and Alex leaned back, staring at the ceiling. The game was getting bigger, and he wasn't sure if he was ready.

~

Parker Davidson

Parker stirred as Kelsey burst into the bedroom, her voice urgent. "Something's going on. Get up."

He and Sydney scrambled out of bed, rubbing sleep from their eyes, and followed her to the living room, where Preston and Leo waited, their faces tense in the dim lantern light.

"What's happening?" Parker asked, his voice rough.

"We've got ideas for dealing with Alex's gang," Preston said, leaning against the wall. "Need your input."

Parker frowned, sitting on the couch. "This couldn't

wait? We're not moving on them for a couple days."

"It's urgent," Leo said, pacing. "I saw Alex at the grocery store, loading up on food and supplies. They're growing—recruiting more members. The bigger they get, the harder they'll be to stop."

Parker nodded, his mind sharpening. "Makes sense. More people, less opposition. I'll draft a spy plan, then a takedown strategy."

He headed to his room to dress, pulling on jeans and a flannel, his leg aching but steadier.

"I've got errands," he told the group. "Be back later."

"I'll come," Leo said, grabbing his jacket.

They left through the neighborhood's south exit, the air cool and heavy with dew.

"Where to?" Leo asked as they walked, their boots crunching on gravel.

"The church," Parker said. "Want to see if the pastor can marry me and Sydney."

Leo raised an eyebrow. "Think he'll do it?"

Parker shrugged, approaching the church, its white paint peeling but its steeple proud. He knocked, and the door cracked open, revealing a middle-aged man with kind eyes.

"Can I help you?" he asked.

"Are you the pastor?" Parker said.

"Pastor Jenkins," the man replied, opening the door wider. "You seeking the Lord?"

"Found Him years ago," Parker said, smiling. "I'm engaged, and we want to get married. Can you help?"

Jenkins nodded. "Sunday work? Come whenever, bring whoever."

"Thank you," Parker said, relief washing over him. "Means a lot."

The door closed and Parker and Leo lingered, the moment sinking in.

"Tomorrow, huh?" Leo said, grinning.

"Yup," Parker said, chuckling. "Let's head back. Gotta tell everyone."

As they walked, Leo's voice softened. "I'm happy for you, man. Wish I had what you and Sydney have."

"You will," Parker said. "Just takes time."

Back home, they found Preston in the living room, Sydney in the kitchen.

"Sydney and I are getting married tomorrow," Parker announced.

Sydney spun around, water bottle in hand. "What? Seriously?"

"Pastor said he'll do it," Parker said, grinning. "Whenever we want, with whoever we want."

"That's amazing!" Sydney said, rushing to hug him, her excitement infectious.

"Bring everyone," Parker said. "It'll be small, but it'll be us."

He grabbed clean clothes and headed to the backyard shower. The cold water stung, washing away days of grime, and he dressed quickly, the air chilly against his damp skin. In the dining room, he set up a board game, cards fanned across the table. "Where's your mom?" he asked Sydney.

"Still sleeping," she said, shuffling cards. "Exhausted from her trip."

Preston and Leo joined them, discussing the gang plan. "We need someone Alex doesn't know," Leo said. "Sam's perfect—your old friend, right?"

"Yeah," Parker said. "But we need to find him and plan this right—escape routes, backups."

After a while, Preston and Leo left for dinner at home. "Keep me posted on any ideas," Parker called.

"Will do," Preston said, waving.

Kelsey and Sydney's voices drifted from the dining room.

"Excited for tomorrow?" Kelsey asked.

"Beyond excited," Sydney said, her voice bright.

Parker lit the camp stove, the flame hissing, and warmed a pot of beans and rice, the savory aroma filling the kitchen. He leaned against the counter, sipping water, then stirred the pot, dividing the food into four bowls.

"Sydney, get your mom for dinner," he said, carrying two bowls to the table.

Sydney nodded, heading upstairs. She returned with Mary, who looked rested but weary, her eyes grateful as she sat.

They ate quietly, the clink of spoons against bowls the only sound, the weight of the day—Alex's gang, the wedding, the invasion—hanging over them.

Parker cleaned the kitchen, scrubbing pots with rainwater, his mind on the plans ahead. *We've got a wedding to pull off, and a gang to stop. No pressure.*

Chapter 21

Alex Carpenter

The warehouse's break room was thick with tension, the air heavy with the smell of burnt coffee and cigarette smoke. Alex leaned forward in his chair, his voice rising as he jabbed a finger at Jack.

"We need the gun store's stock for the recruits. Too many guns is better than not enough!"

Jack crossed his arms, his jaw tight. "We've got plenty, Alex. Why risk it? If the owners are there, we're dead—no question."

"They're dead!" Alex shouted, slamming his fist on the table, rattling a stack of empty mugs. "It's not robbing, it's borrowing."

Hector burst in, his boots scuffing the concrete floor, his face etched with irritation. "What's with the yelling? You've woken half the crew!"

"Jack thinks hitting the gun store's a bad idea," Alex snapped, glaring. "We need those guns for the new guys."

Jack threw up his hands. "We're not short on firepower, idiot. And if the owners are alive, we're screwed."

Hector yawned, rubbing his eyes. "I'm with Jack, Alex. Too risky."

Alex's face flushed, his voice sharp. "I heard fifteen gunshots from that store days ago. Whoever was in there—owners, customers—is gone."

Hector raised an eyebrow. "And if it was a customer who got shot, not the owners?"

"Only one way to find out," Alex said, flopping into his office chair, the springs creaking. "We go."

"Not me," Jack said, storming out, the door banging shut.

"Me, neither," Hector added, following him.

"Screw you both," Alex yelled after them, his voice echoing in the empty office.

He stood, his pulse racing, and strode to the warehouse's back door. Outside, a warm breeze carried the scent of dust and wild grass. He took a deep breath, calming himself, and returned to his desk. A folder labeled "Recruits" caught his eye, its edges worn. He opened it, scanning pages of names and details—ages, skills, backgrounds.

One caught his attention: a nineteen-year-old with medical training. *That's new*, he thought, setting it aside. He sorted through the rest, crumpling rejects and tucking potentials back into the folder, his mind churning with plans.

The warehouse was quiet, too quiet. He headed to the break room, expecting to find the crew, but it was empty, the air stale with lingering smoke. At the unloading bay, he found them gathered outside, leaning against cars, debating recruits.

"Thought you all bailed," Alex said, stepping into the sunlight.

"Just talking," Hector said, kicking a pebble. "Which recruits do you like?"

"A few," Alex said, shrugging. "Still deciding. Need good ones."

"Take your time," Hector said. "So, the gun store—what's the deal?"

"We're going," Alex said, his tone final. "Three cars, two per car. I'm in."

Hector groaned. "Guess I'm stuck then."

"Let's move," Alex said, nodding to the cars. "Before someone else gets the same idea."

Six of them piled into three sedans, leaving a skeleton crew to guard the warehouse. As they drove down the rutted dirt road, the garage doors clanging shut behind them, Alex stared out the window.

What if we control everything? he wondered. The power to dictate trade—guns, luxury goods, tobacco—would make them untouchable, but the police loomed large.

We need those recruits trained fast. Take out the cops, maybe even the mayor. His thoughts darkened as they hit the main road, the car bouncing over potholes.

At the gun store, two officers stood out front, their AR-15s glinting in the sun. Alex's stomach sank. Hector parked, and Alex stepped out, forcing a casual tone.

"What's going on, officer?"

"Store's been cleaned out," the officer said, his grip tightening on his rifle as the others exited the cars.

"Hardly anything left—a couple boxes of ammo, that's it."

Alex's jaw clenched. "When? Who did it?"

"No clue," the officer said, shaking his head. "Saw Parker Davidson and his friends here a few days ago, grabbing ammo. Maybe guns, too."

Alex shot Hector a look, his blood boiling.

"Thanks," he said, climbing back into the car. "Parker Davidson," he muttered. "Of course."

"Where to?" Hector asked, starting the engine.

"Back to the hideout," Alex said. "We'll hit a gun store in the next town."

As they drove, Alex's mind raced. Parker's arming a group. That's why he took everything. He recalled the confrontation days ago—Peter and Xavier's deaths, Parker's defiance.

A nearby town, an hour west, had a hunting store with rifles and shotguns. It wasn't ideal, but it'd do. Back at the warehouse, Alex called a meeting, the crew gathered in the break room, their faces a mix of exhaustion and anticipation.

"The gun store here's empty," he said, pacing. "Parker Davidson's group beat us to it. There's a hunting store an hour west. We hit it, grab everything—rifles, shotguns, ammo."

"Why not just take Parker's group out?" Zack asked, leaning back in his chair.

"They're experienced, probably bigger than us," Alex said. "We need better gear first."

"When do we go?" Jack asked, his tone reluctant.

"Soon," Alex said. "Before dark. Take the fourth car."

The crew scattered, grabbing gear—backpacks, crowbars, empty crates. Alex climbed into the backseat of Hector's car, sprawling across it. "Why back there?" Hector asked, starting the engine.

"Nap time," Alex said, closing his eyes.

He dozed off, the car's hum lulling him, until Hector slammed on the brakes, jolting him awake.

"What's going on?"

"Some guy jumped in the road," Hector said, pointing to a disheveled man waving frantically.

Alex grabbed his pistol and stepped out, his boots crunching gravel. "Who do you think you are, stopping us?"

"I need help," the man stammered, his face bleak. "Been walking days. My wife's in that town—"

"Move, or your wife's a widow," Alex snapped, raising his pistol.

The man stumbled aside, and Alex climbed back in.

"Go," he told Hector. They drove the final twelve minutes, parking outside the hunting store, its sign faded but intact. Inside, a few rifles hung on the wall, but Alex knew the real haul was in the back. A grizzled man emerged when the bell jingled, his eyes narrowing.

"Can I help you?" he asked, his hand hovering near his hip.

"Everything," Alex said, his voice cold. "Every gun, all the ammo. Now."

The man tilted his head. "What do I get?"

Alex stepped closer, his hand on his pistol. "Everything. Move."

The man hesitated, then shrugged. "Not unless I get something."

Alex drew his pistol, aiming it at the man's chest. "Seven against one. Your call."

The man raised his hands, muttering, and headed to the back, hauling out crates of rifles, shotguns, and ammo.

Alex watched him, finger near the trigger, while the crew loaded the cars, the clatter of metal echoing. When the last crate was out, Alex demanded the keys. The man handed them over, and Alex locked him in the back room, tossing the keys on the counter.

"Let's go," he said, striding out.

They passed the begging man again, ignoring his pleas, and returned to the warehouse, pulling the cars into the indoor parking area. The crew unloaded, stacking guns and ammo on shelves, the air thick with gun oil and dust.

Alex cataloged the haul—twenty rifles, ten shotguns, thousands of rounds—his pen scratching furiously. *Recruits next, he thought. Then we take down the cops and Parker's crew.*

~

Parker Davidson

Parker woke to Sydney's excited shaking, her eyes bright with anticipation.

"Come on, it's our wedding day!" she said, practically bouncing as she left to make breakfast.

Parker rubbed his eyes, a grin spreading despite his

groggy state. His leg ached, a dull reminder of the stabbing, but he swung out of bed, steadying himself against the wall.

In the kitchen, Sydney cracked eggs into a skillet, the sizzle filling the air with a savory aroma.

"Didn't think you'd be this excited," he teased, leaning on the counter.

"You're not?" she shot back, stirring the eggs, her engagement ring glinting.

"I am," he said, chuckling. "Just tired, and my leg's still whining."

"Take it easy," she said, her tone softening. "No heroics today."

He nodded, heading upstairs to wake Kelsey. He tapped her shoulder gently, the room dim with morning light. "Breakfast's almost ready. Want some?"

She nodded, stretching. "Be down soon."

Back in the kitchen, Sydney had moved on to pancakes, the sweet batter smell mingling with the eggs. Parker set the table, plates clinking, and let Nala in from the backyard, her fur damp with dew. She jumped up, her paws warm in his hands, and he tossed her toy across the room, her excited barks echoing.

Sydney called that the pancakes were done, and Kelsey and Mary descended, their faces bright despite the early hour.

"Morning," Kelsey said, sitting as they all served themselves eggs and pancakes, the food a rare treat after weeks of rationing. They ate in companionable silence, savoring each bite. After, they agreed to clean the house before the wedding. Parker tackled the kitchen, scrubbing pots with rainwater, then moved to his bedroom, straightening the cluttered space.

The guns in the garage nagged at him—too exposed. He hauled them to the basement, box by box, his leg protesting but holding. Rifles, pistols, and ammo crates filled the shelves, their weight reassuring but hidden. *No one's stealing these now,* he thought, wiping sweat from his brow.

In his room, he found Sydney getting ready, her dress simple but elegant, scavenged from a neighbor's attic. He dressed too, pulling on a clean shirt and jeans, the fabric stiff but fresh. In the dining room, he grabbed the radio, clicking it on.

"Preston, Chris, Leo—you guys coming?"

"Coming to what?" Leo teased, laughing.

"The wedding," Parker said, grinning. "We want you there."

"Getting ready now," Preston said. "Ten minutes, meet in the driveway."

"Will do," Parker said, switching off the radio.

He checked on Sydney, who was adjusting her hair. "Ready?" he asked.

"Almost," she said, smiling nervously.

He leashed Nala, her tail wagging furiously, and handed the leash to Kelsey, who joined them with Mary, both dressed neatly.

"I'm happy for you," Kelsey said, hugging him tightly.

"Thanks, Mom," Parker said, his throat tight. "Glad you're here."

They stepped outside, finding Preston, Chris, Leo, Angelina, and Bella waiting in the driveway, their faces bright with anticipation.

"Let's go get married," Parker called, his voice steady despite the butterflies in his stomach.

They walked together through the neighborhood's south exit, the air warm and thick with the scent of blooming honeysuckle. Parker's excitement grew with each step, his hand brushing Sydney's, her ring cool against his fingers. *This is it. The rest of our lives.*

The church loomed ahead, its doors open, sunlight streaming through the stained-glass windows, casting colored patterns on the pews. They filed in, taking the front row, while Parker and Sydney approached the altar. Pastor Jenkins emerged, his smile warm, his robes slightly wrinkled but dignified.

Parker glanced at Kelsey and Mary, both wiping tears, their pride evident.

The pastor's voice rang clear. "Do you, Parker, take Sydney to be your lawfully wedded wife?"

"I do," Parker said, his voice steady, his eyes locked on Sydney's.

"And do you, Sydney, take Parker to be your lawfully wedded husband?"

"I do," she said, her voice trembling with joy.

"Then, without further ado," the pastor said, "I pronounce you husband and wife. You may kiss the bride."

Parker pulled Sydney close, sealing their promise in a world unraveling around them. Parker and Sydney stayed a while longer than everyone else, taking a slow walk back to the house. Everyone else insisted on heading out ahead of them.

As they walked up the driveway they could see the inside of the house lit up by candles. Inside everyone was gathered up, with food cooked and placed on the table.

"Congrats!" Everyone yelled.

They both cracked smiles. "Thank you, guys."

"Figured you guys deserve some kind of party. It's only fair."

They spent the night together, as one big family, celebrating Parker and Sydney, but also how far they'd all come. Since the EMP started, life ahead was unknown, even surviving a week was a feat.

Everyone talked about their lives before the EMP. As the night wore on, everyone began heading to bed, leaving Parker and Sydney. They talked a little while longer before heading off to bed for the night.

Chapter 22

Parker Davidson

Parker grabbed the radio and clicked the call button. "Hey, Preston, Leo, I'm going to get Sam so we can talk with him."

"Do you want us to come with you?" Preston asked a moment later.

"If you want. Meet me outside in a couple of minutes, and we will head over to his house."

"Okay."

Parker shut the radio off and clipped it to his pocket. He took a deep breath. *If he says yes, then it's one step closer to stopping Alex. If he says no, then back to square one. At that point, would we even be able to figure something out fast enough?*

Parker grabbed his backpack and pistol off the dining room table. He put his pistol in its holster with a satisfying click and approached the door.

Just as he reached for the door, Sydney's voice behind him brought him to a solid stop. "Where are you off to so early?"

Parker turned to see Sydney, "We're going to pitch the spy operation to Sam and see what he thinks."

"Be careful."

"Always," he said, forcing a grin before stepping onto the porch. Across the street he could see Preston in his driveway.

"Just in time," Parker said. "Ready to go?"

"Yup," Preston said, adjusting his backpack as they started down the sidewalk. "Is Leo ready?"

"Not yet, but he's on the way to Sam's," Parker explained, beginning the walk to Leo's house.

The air was still and quiet, aside from the faint chirp of birds or the hum of cicadas.

"So, how do you think this is gonna go?"

"Well, he's always been the cautious type. The likelihood that he says yes is honestly low in my opinion. He never liked to take risks back in high school, so we'll have to see."

"What's the likelihood he says no?"

"No idea. When it comes to situations like this and asking for his help, there's no telling what he'll say."

They reached Leo's house, one of the oldest in the neighborhood. The paint was peeling, the shingles all cracked. Parker knocked on the front door.

Leo's mom answered the door with a sour look, anger in her voice. "What do you want, Parker?"

"Is Leo ready?" Parker asked, remaining calm, despite her obvious anger.

Preston raised an eyebrow. "She's... different."

"Always has been," Parker explained, stepping off of the porch. "Some days she's fine, others, not so much."

The door swung open as Leo stepped outside. "Sorry about that. Mom had me cleaning the kitchen top to bottom. Wish I got to move out before this EMP."

"Typical mom." Preston joked.

"Let's get going," Parker said.

After the trek to Sam's house—winding through the

streets filled with cars and abandoned houses—they knocked at the door.

As the door creaked open Sam asked, "Who's there? What's going on? Why are you here?"

"We need to talk," Parker explained, pushing past him to the dusty living room.

Sam joined them after shutting the door. "What's all this about?"

"Alex Carpenter," Parker began, sinking into the couch. "His gang was behind most of the crime before the EMP, and now I fear they're going to take over."

Sam sat in the chair across from him. "And? I stayed away from him in high school, but I was friendly, so he likely won't do anything to me."

"That's why you're perfect for this operation; we need someone to give us intel on his gang, anything we can use to take them down."

Sam's eyes widened. "No. That's insane! If he were to find out why I was there I'd be dead on sight, no questions asked."

Preston raised his hands. "I get that. But, it's the only way. In return, we'll keep you in any, and all the supplies you could need to live through everything."

Sam paced the living room, scratching his head. "Let me think about it. It's a huge risk."

Parker nodded. "Alright, just please let me know soon so we can decide what's next."

Sam nodded and gestured for them to leave.

After they stepped outside they stood for a minute. "That didn't go as planned."

Preston shook his head. "No it didn't, but we'll get an answer eventually."

As they passed Leo's house, they said their goodbyes and parted ways.

"Well, get home. If he says yes then we have a busy week ahead of us."

Preston nodded, waving as he crossed the street to his house. Parker went inside his own and dropped his things at the door, partially upset with how things went.

Kelsey appeared at the bottom of the stairs, a curious look on her face. "So, what did Sam say?"

"Says it's risky and needs a day or two to think," Parker said, grabbing a stale granola bar from the box.

"That only means we're losing time," Kelsey said, sitting in the dining room.

"What do you think I told him when he told us that? I just hope he makes up his mind quick."

"I hope so, too."

Parker sank onto the couch, reaching for the plant book he left on the coffee table. With winter a few months away, food security was something they all had on their minds. The likelihood of running out in the middle of winter was high, and that was the last thing they needed. The solution he'd come up with was a small greenhouse they could use throughout the winter.

He went outside, Nala trailing behind him. He looked over the yard, finding the best spot would be the corner opposite of the chicken coop. He went to the garage and grabbed a tape measure to see how much space he had to work with. He wrote down the measurements before heading back inside to sketch out plans. They had a stack of hanging pots in the garage from their old house. He found a way to work them into the plan, allowing them extra plantable soil.

He brought three ideas to his mom for her opinion.

"Mom, here are a couple of ideas I came up with for greenhouses. Which one looks best to you?" he asked, handing her the notebook.

She looked over the three designs and picked one out. "That one looks like it would be the easiest to manage and the most efficient."

"That's what I was thinking, too, but I wanted to hear your input," Parker told her.

"The others look good too, but that one seems it'd be the best for quantity."

Parker nodded before walking out of the room. He went downstairs and found Sydney sitting on the couch. "Good shower?"

"Cold, but great," she explained.

"I thought of something new. I'm going to get a greenhouse built here in the next few days so we can be ready for winter."

"Winter isn't for another," she thought, squinting her eyes, "five-ish months, though."

"I understand that, but I'd rather be ready for it than not prepared."

"Well, if you need help, I'm happy to," she said, returning interest to her book.

As evening fell Parker began cooking dinner for the household, setting the pot off of the heat and on the table for everyone to eat.

"So, mom. Have you thought about your co-workers back in Washington? Think they made it home?"

Kelsey jumped up from the table. "That reminds me."

She ran upstairs and quickly returned with a hard-shelled case. "They gave me a radio and antenna to contact them."

"Why'd they give you a radio?"

She shrugged. "I don't know, but there is a chance they know more about what's happening across the country. Top military personnel, they have to know more than we do."

She turned the radio on and started scanning the channels, though the five-foot antenna likely wouldn't reach Washington without other antennas between them. She kept spinning the dial, searching channels, until one began to make noise.

Hello? Is anyone out there? This is George Harmen. I am located in Washington. Is anyone alive out there? Things are getting hairy up here. Soldiers are setting up posts across the state. They won't provide any information, and I'm worried about what's to come. Does anyone know what's going on? If you hear this, I beg of you, please respond.

Kelsey looked at Parker wide eyed. "That's my boss."

"Are you going to radio back?"

She looked back at the radio and held the green button. "Hello, George Harmen. Can you hear this?"

A moment of silence passed. *Yes, I read you. Who are you? More importantly, where are you? Are you safe?*

"I'm...I'm Kelsey Davidson. I made it back to Tennessee," she spoke into the radio.

Kel...Kelsey... Is that really you? I'm glad you made it back to Tennessee. You were supposed to contact me when you made it back, why didn't you?

"Things have been really bad here. We are facing fears of a gang wreaking havoc across Nashville, and a foreign military invasion." Kelsey explained.

Jesus, maybe that explains the soldiers. HISS! down there? How long did it take for you to make it back? HISS! Make the journey? Static began to take over the message.

"Can you repeat that? Static took over."

Nothing but static came over the radio. Kelsey set it down.

"As much as I hate to say this, I miss him. I would like to see him again."

"What do you think he said when the static took over?"

Parker asked her, trying to figure it out himself.

"My guess is as good as yours. 'Down there' and 'make the journey'. Do you think he wants to get down here?" Kelsey asked, standing up to go back inside.

Parker shrugged. "That's my best guess. I don't know what else he might be trying to say, maybe asking if Mary made it, but who knows."

They went back inside and sat back down. "So, anything?"

"Yeah, George has been trying to get in contact with people for days. Towards the end, though, static began to take over the message," Kelsey explained, taking a bite of food, her face turning bitter when she found it was cold.

Parker ate his food while Mary and his mom talked; though he didn't enjoy the cold food, it was better than nothing. Once he was finished, he cleaned up and sat back down.

"Listen, tomorrow, first thing in the morning, try to contact him again. Maybe it will be an uninterrupted transmission this time," Parker suggested.

"I'll try, but I doubt it will be better than just now," Kelsey said, taking her plate to the kitchen. Once everyone was finished eating and the house was clean, they all went to bed.

Parker tried to go to sleep right away but wasn't able to. He lay awake thinking of what the next step was with handling the gang. After he cleared his mind, he was finally able to go to sleep.

~

Alex Carpenter

Alex jolted awake to frantic banging on his office door, his heart pounding. He stumbled to the door, yanking it open to find Hector and Jack, their faces pale.

"What do you morons want?" he snapped, rubbing sleep from his eyes.

"Sorry, boss," Hector said, trying to catch his breath. "Four cops are coming this way. They're geared up, looking for a fight."

Alex groaned. "Right after I wake up? Get everyone ready. I'll be right down."

Alex retreated into his office and grabbed his pistol from the top drawer on the right. He then grabbed the rifle that was in the corner behind the door. He left the office, slamming the door behind him. Downstairs he found about half of his gang waiting for him to tell them what to do. He peered around the corner and counted four officers all marching along the path.

His pulse raced as he and his crew crossed the path, taking cover behind some bushes. His heart almost beat out of his chest as the officers raised their rifles in their direction.

They heard us! he thought. He raised his gun, waiting. As soon as the officers lowered their rifles he motioned for everyone to take aim.

He took the first shot, breaking the awkward silence surrounding the area. It struck the officer in the chest. He didn't go down, he merely staggered back before aiming back at him.

Body armor. More shots filled the air, the majority from his crew. Once the officers were down they finished the job and dumped the bodies into the bushes.

"They'll come looking real quick. We need to be ready to go after the whole police force."

"We need to make sure these four are hidden. They will most definitely walk more guys this way looking for 'em," Zach pointed out.

Everyone nodded. Once the bodies were hidden, they went back inside the warehouse.

Alex called everyone together for a quick meeting. "Okay, so, after today, I think we need to put together a watch team. We will have watches, switching bi-hourly. I'll set up a schedule, and we will get right to it. I'm tired of these police ruining our plans."

Alex returned to his office and set his things down, his rifle back in the corner and his pistol back in the drawer. He flopped into his chair and almost fell backward, but somehow caught himself.

He grabbed his notebook and started writing out watch plans. He put everyone onto a watch at some point in the day. Once the schedule was finished, he took it to the breakroom and set it down, knowing everyone would look at it when they could.

He went to get Zach and Gavin so they could start their watch shift. Once they were sent out, Alex returned to his office and sat down. He looked around, trying to figure out what to do, and decided to read through his inventory.

Chapter 23

Parker Davidson

Parker climbed out of bed, his leg giving a faint sign of pain. He went downstairs and found Kelsey awake.

"Have you tried the radio yet?"

"Not yet. I was waiting for you so that you can hear, too."

He nodded. "Well, let's go try it."

They set it up outside at the table and began scanning channels, trying to find the one they were on last night. "George? Hello, are you awake?"

HISS! Sey? Kelsey, I'm glad to hear your voice again. Things are getting bad up here. The US troops are on the move and have made a camp at our research facility. I need to get out of here.

"Okay." Kelsey took a deep breath. "Do you think you can make it down to Nashville on your own?"

"You're going to let him come down here?" Parker asked her, shocked.

"He's my boss. I can't just let him die. He might be a good asset to our group anyway." She shot back.

I might be able to. It'll be a week or two, but I can try. What if you meet me halfway? I know you have a working vehicle. I'll get halfway there, and you can come get me.

HISS! Ease.

"I'll think about it. Just get your things packed. If there truly is a foreign invasion, you need to leave before they reach Everett. Just work your way southeast, and get away from the coast as fast as you can. Check in with me around sundown."

Okay, thank you. I'll be back on this thing around then. Be safe.

Kelsey shut the radio off. "Either way, he could be valuable to us. He has connections that can help us greatly; just be open-minded."

"Fine, but last I checked, George wasn't exactly a stand-up guy," Parker exclaimed, going back inside.

He got dressed, ready to begin work on the greenhouse. He grabbed his notebook with the plans and brought it with him to the garage. He yanked the large door open, the light quickly streamed in.

He set up the saw horses in the backyard and set the first 2x4 on it. He began to saw it when Sydney came outside. "Working hard this early?"

"Mhm, it needs to get done, so figured I'd start. It's getting hot, though."

"It is really hot. Let me know if you need anything," she told him before going back inside.

After an hour he had all of the 2x4s cut, the pile filling the corner where the greenhouse would be going. He cleaned everything up before heading inside for a break from the heat.

"How is the greenhouse coming out?" Mary asked from the living room.

"Eh, I got all of the wood cut, so I'm part of the way there. The only thing I'm still trying to work out is the clear plastic that surrounds it."

"Hm. You could use plastic wrap, but that wouldn't be super durable."

"I know, I thought about that one, too, but I would need

to replace it nearly every day, so it's not sustainable," Parker told her. "Wait, the clear shower curtains."

"Those would be perfect. No one needs them anymore anyway. Showers don't work," Mary exclaimed. "Good thinking."

"Thank you. Well, I'll gather the ones from the bathrooms and the extra ones we have; hopefully, that'll be enough," Parker said, jumping up from the chair.

He went upstairs and grabbed the shower curtain off the rod. Kelsey came in after hearing all of the noise.

"Parker, what are you doing?"

"I'm using the curtains for the greenhouse; they will work as the plastic, so light can still get in."

"Smart. Will we have enough?"

"We should. I hope we still have a few new ones that I can use, too."

He brought the six curtains he had gathered out to the yard and dropped them by the structure. He began to nail them, forming walls and a roof. He trimmed the excess off and cleaned up, happy to be done and get out of the heat.

Kelsey, I've made it just outside of Everett. I've been heading south along the coast for a couple of hours or so. There are warships sitting on the coast, no more than a quarter mile away. The further south I get, the more Humvees and soldiers there are. What should I do?

Parker ran upstairs and to find his mom in her room. "Hey, George just got on the radio, you need to come down here."

"What'd he say?" she asked, setting down the box she was sorting through.

"Uh.. Something along the lines of he's been heading south down the coast for a couple of hours, warships no more than, I think he said, a quarter mile off the coast. And soldiers everywhere."

Kelsey ran downstairs and outside to the radio. She picked it up and started talking. "George, what's going on? I didn't hear the message."

I've been heading down the coast for a couple of hours. There's warships on the coast and soldiers everywhere. Wait. Sir, you need to leave this area now! W... Why? Just go, go east, get out of here! HISSS!

"Argh, what is going on? It sounded like he was getting yelled at by soldiers. That's at least what I would assume."

"It's okay. We'll contact him in a little bit. I'm sure he's fine," Parker told her.

"I know he will be fine. I just want to know what's going on. Everything is chaotic every time we talk to him."

She got up and went back inside; Parker followed her in and went to his room to find Sydney reading her book.

"How'd the greenhouse come out?"

"Good, shower curtains work as well as the plastic would, but we'll have to see how well they trap heat," Parker explained. "Mom and I just tried talking to George. She missed a message from him, and when he explained what was going on, he was getting yelled at by soldiers telling him to leave."

"Whoa, things must be getting bad out there, huh?" Sydney asked, setting her book down.

"Yeah, he said the warships that my mom saw on her journey back are about a quarter mile off of the coast."

"That's not a good sign. I wonder what military this is."

"Me, too!" Parker exclaimed. "I'm going to make some eggs. Do you want some?"

"Um, sure. I'll take some, and I'll be out in a couple of minutes."

"Alright, no rush; it'll take a couple of minutes," Parker said, getting up and heading for the kitchen.

Parker whipped up some eggs and plated them for him and Sydney. While they ate, they discussed the threat of the ships, them being that close meant an invasion wasn't only possible, it was already happening.

~

George Harmen

"Sir, you need to leave this area now!" a soldier approached him and yelled in his face.

"W... Why?" George stammered, folding up the portable antenna.

"Just go, go east, get out of here!" the soldier barked, pointing.

As George started going the way the soldier had pointed, he passed multiple groups of soldiers running. When he came across a Humvee with a soldier standing by it, he took his chance to find out what was happening.

"S... Sir?" he asked, coming up behind the soldier.

The soldier jumped and turned to face him. "Who are you?"

"I was just told to go east, but I want to know what's happening."

"Listen, I don't have time for this. All I'm going to tell you is we are at war," the soldier told him before returning to what he was doing.

As George walked away, he thought *If we're at war, who are we at war with? Are any of our allies going to come help?*

All George knew was that he needed to get east and somewhere safe so he could contact Kelsey. He continued walking the highway, which was filled with military vehicles. He weaved his way through the many vehicles until eventually reaching the end of them.

He looked back to see an overview of what he had just walked through. It was a field at the end of the highway, filled with Humvees and other vehicles. Hundreds of soldiers were running about, and warships were in the distance.

He continued walking, figuring it would be best to get out of an active warzone. *I hope this doesn't get any worse. And please, God, let me get to Nashville safely.*

Hours of walking later, George looked up to see the sun quickly setting, though he knew he needed to get a couple more hours of walking in before stopping. George knew that he should've left with Kelsey or Mary, but deep inside him, he thought the power would come back on and work would continue. However, after nearly three weeks without power, he finally decided to hoof it and get somewhere safe.

George had no family and nowhere to go, he'd never had a home of his own, just lived wherever work took him. He had an apartment down in New Mexico, where their company's main office was, but he hardly spent time there. That's why he thought of going to Tennessee with Kelsey. He figured it'd be his best bet for survival, especially with what he had just seen on the coast.

George continued walking for another hour before stopping as it got dark. A group of cars lay ahead, he set up camp between them, hopefully granting him cover from any looters walking the highway. He looked around every couple of minutes, paranoid of seeing people. He opened his backpack and tried to see if he had any food that he had forgotten about. Nothing.

George had never been the 'prepare for the end' type, but he had known people like that his entire life. This was one of the times that he wished he was that type of person. He knew he would need food and water to reach the halfway point between him and Nashville. He pulled out the radio and antenna and set it up so he could try to talk with Kelsey.

"Kelsey? Hello? Can you hear me?" he asked, hoping she was near the radio.

George, thank God you're okay. What happened earlier? I was worried. HISS!

"Um, well, the soldiers were telling me I had to leave right away. I learned that we are at war. Did you know that?" George explained.

Ugh, yes, I knew that. I know more about this than you. There was a pause. *I can't believe I thought you knew more than I did,* she said, barely audible to George.

"What was that last part? I... Didn't hear it." he asked.

Oh, nothing. I'm sorry. I was talking to Parker. Well, where are you now? Do you know? And how long do you think it will take to make it to South Dakota? At least the western border; that's the rough halfway point.

"What is it, maybe a thousand miles? Ugh, I can maybe make it in a few weeks, even less if I find a car or can get a ride." George told her.

It's going to be hard to get a ride—I had a hard time doing it—but a car may be a little more manageable. Though some people might not be willing to give theirs up. If I were you, I would get to a city and find an older car—I'm talking pre-2000s—and siphon gas. It's a long shot one would be sitting around, but there is always a chance.

"Any specific type of vehicle? Like, car or truck?" George asked.

No, as long as it is a working vehicle that you can easily fuel with siphoned gas, it will work. Just do that in the morning. I'll talk to you around noon.

"O...Okay, that will do. I'll talk to you then," George said, turning the radio off. "Oh boy, let's hope I can find a working car," George mumbled to himself.

George packed the radio up to make it easy to head out in the morning. He set his pack up like a pillow and lay down. It wasn't comfortable, but it would have to do.

George woke up the next morning, his neck aching from lying on his backpack. He could hear footsteps on the smashed glass on the other side of the car. He peered under the car and found four people walking past the car.

"Ha, that kid was shaking in his boots." One of the people exclaimed, audibly reloading a rifle.

George looked through the window of one of the cars and saw four figures. He quickly ducked down when one of them looked in his direction.

"Did you guys see that?" a woman asked. "There was something behind that car right there."

George's heart began to speed up.

"No, it was probably just an animal," Another answered.

"You're probably right," the woman said. "How long until we get to Seattle?"

As the people went further away, their voices became harder to hear. Once their voices were out of earshot, George looked through one of the car windows again to ensure it was clear. He grabbed his backpack and started down the highway, eastbound. After a couple of minutes of walking, his stomach began to rumble, causing him to worry.

He hoped there was somewhere he could get food soon to help him, otherwise he might have more significant problems than no car. As he approached a small no-name town, he found there was a gas station right at the edge. He walked through the pumps and to the shop.

The place was trashed, candy wrappers littered the floor, and something sticky covering it, catching his shoes. He walked down the aisles and grabbed just about anything he could. He shoved everything into his backpack before going to the refrigerators. He found two lone water bottles in one of the refrigerators. He drank the first one, quenching his thirst enough to keep going. The other found its way into his backpack, as well as the two protein bars and small bag of jerky he found.

Once he was satisfied with what he had found, he left the store and went walking down the town's main road, keeping an eye out for older vehicles, praying he would find one that would work.

There weren't many people outside, though there were a few, but none of them cared to make contact with him. He looked around the town, mostly seeing newer SUVs and trucks resting in driveways and on the road. As he was reaching the end of the town, he saw an older-looking car on the street in front of a house.

He walked over, examining the car, an old Ford Fusion, just what he was looking for. He looked around and climbed the porch, knocking on the door. He received no answer. Trying the knob, he found it was unlocked.

He carefully shut the door behind him and walked through the house to the kitchen. He looked around and found multiple trophy mounts of deer, elk, and a couple of other animals he didn't know the names of. He continued looking around and, when he reached the kitchen, saw a bear skull on the fridge. He started thinking about whether the owner was possibly home, just asleep.

He opened every drawer one by one until he found one with keys. He grabbed a set with a Ford logo and shut the drawer. He eased his way back through the house to the front door, being careful not to make too much noise due to the creaky floor.

As he opened the front door a voice behind him called, "What the hell do you think you're doing!"

Chapter 24

Parker Davidson

Parker woke up and looked out of the window. He saw the sun just starting to peek over the horizon. Next to him, Sydney was cuddled up with Nala. He crawled out of bed and went to the living room, took another look outside and admired the sunrise.

He went to the kitchen and whipped up a serving of eggs for breakfast and quickly ate. He then went back to his bedroom, changed into his clothes for the day, and went outside.

He walked down the driveway and along the sidewalk. He walked laps around the block for an hour, wanting some exercise.

As he climbed the driveway to head back inside, he heard heavy steps behind him.

He turned around to see Anna.

"Anna, what are you doing back?" He took another look at her. Her face was red as if she'd been crying, and her hair was a mess. "Anna?"

"They were all dead. Dead!" she yelled, stumbling up the driveway another step before falling to her knees.

Parker ran over and knelt next to her.

"Anna, are you okay?" he asked as he eased her backpack off of her shoulders. He looked around, not wanting to draw attention. "Anna, let's get you inside."

She stood up, and Parker grabbed her backpack and helped her inside. He set the backpack in the dining room and went upstairs.

Entering Kelsey's bedroom, he lightly shook her awake. "Mom, Anna's back."

"Wh...What, Anna left days ago," Kelsey told him, swatting at his poking hand.

"Mom, she came back. She won't tell me anything," Parker explained.

"I'll be down in a minute," she told him, sitting up.

Parker left the room and went downstairs.

Kelsey came down behind him. "When did Anna get here?"

"Not important, but she got here and broke down. I... I don't know what to do. She won't say anything other than everyone's dead."

Parker led her to the living room, where they found Anna lying on the couch, still crying.

Preston came in, having been drawn by the commotion. "What happened to her? I thought she went back to Georgia."

"She did. She showed up like fifteen minutes ago and immediately broke down into tears."

"Did she say anything before she did... that."

"She said they were all dead. My only thought is that when she got back she found everyone dead. But I'm not sure."

"Only logical explanation, but we need to get her some food and water, she's probably been walking for days to make it back," Kelsey explained.

"Agreed," Parker and Preston both said.

"If she is going to stay here, then we need to figure out sleeping arrangements."

"We have a cot we could set up in the basement, but that's about it." Parker exclaimed, "This place is filling up fast!"

"I guess that will have to do, but I need to know what happened when she got home. I'm curious," Kelsey said, glancing behind her.

She went back to the living room and knelt next to the couch. "Anna, are you okay? Do you need to talk about what happened?"

Anna sort of peeked her head up. "Please."

"Alright, well, what happened?" Kelsey asked.

"I got home after walking for a couple of days. I knocked on my parent's door, and there wasn't an answer. So I went inside to the kitchen, and their bodies were on the ground," she explained, sobbing the whole time.

"Oh, my God, that's horrible. Is there anything you need?" Sydney said, trying her best to console her.

"Well... I was sort of hoping I could stay here with you guys again. I'll help with anything you need," Anna replied.

Kelsey thought about it, looking at Parker. "Sure, but you need to rest. I'm sure you are tired after walking back."

"Yes, I need sleep," Anna said.

Kelsey stood up and joined Parker and Preston in the kitchen. "We'll let her be for now, and set up the cot and stuff later. Right now, she needs to rest and take her mind off things."

Everyone nodded before splitting across the house. Parker followed Preston outside, and they talked for a little bit before saying their goodbyes. Parker came back inside and found Kelsey sitting in the dining room.

"Mom, should we try and talk with George?" Parker asked.

"We could, but, I think he will be driving so he probably won't have the radio set up," Kelsey replied.

"Oh, well, then maybe we can do it tonight or something," Parker said.

Kelsey nodded before heading upstairs to start working on more cleaning. Parker began to get bored and decided he was going to shoot his bow. He went out to the garage and grabbed their target, carried it to the backyard and set it by the wastewater corner of the yard. He went back inside and upstairs to get his bow from their new storage room.

Once his bow was set up he left the room and bumped into Kelsey.

"What are you doing?"

"I figured I'd go shoot for a bit; I need something to do," Parker told her. "Maybe I can use it to hunt and get us some fresh meat."

"Good luck. Shoot straight."

~

George Harmen

"Turn around slowly," the voice said, "Keep your hands visible."

George's heart sped up. He began thinking, trying to figure out why he was doing what he was doing. He began to turn around, keeping his hands out to his side. Once he had finished his turn, he could see a man with a long beard, baseball cap on, cigarette hanging out of his mouth, and shotgun in his hands.

"Now, why don't you explain to me why you are in my house," he said, his voice hoarse.

"We...Well, I'm trying to get back to Tennessee, and, and, I need a car," George explained to the man.

"No excuse to break into my house and steal a car, now is it? So, why don't you take that backpack off, and give it to me. You will be getting comfortable in the basement," the man explained, lowering the shotgun.

"But, but, I need to get home," George said.

"Well, you should have thought about that before breaking into my house. Now give me the pack, or I'll get it myself," the man told him. "And you's don't want me to get it myself."

George accepted defeat. The second he opened the door, he knew he was making a bad decision. He went through with it, and now he was paying the price. He tossed the pack on the floor at the man's feet. "Please be careful with it; there is a radio in it."

"Listen, buddy, radios don't work. So, no, I won't be careful," he told him.

"It does work; it was Faraday caged," George told him, beginning to get irritated.

"Oh, really? Interesting. Well, get over here and empty your pockets," the man said, using the shotgun to guide him.

George cautiously walked over and began to pull things out of his pockets, dropping them all into the man's large hands. The last two things he pulled out were his phone and wallet. Why he was still carrying his phone, he hardly knew himself.

"Alright, go over there. That door is to the basement. Here is a lantern. Enjoy and get comfortable," the man directed, jabbing the shotgun barrel into his back.

George opened the door and began to walk down the steps leading to the basement. Upon reaching the bottom, he noticed a small amount of light from small windows high on the walls. He turned the lantern on and walked around the basement, exploring what was there.

He found it was mostly just a main room and a small

storage area. He went into the storage area and found it to be mostly empty, aside from a couple of random things scattered around. He left and returned to the main room, which was empty. He leaned against a wall and slid down.

He sat in silence for a couple of hours, listening. He could hear the man talking to someone, whom he assumed was his wife.

"This guy has nothing of worth, aside from the radio."

"Shouldn't we let him talk to his family, or whoever he is trying to get home to? Maybe they will come get him, and then we won't have to deal with him," a woman's voice said.

"I guess. Go get him," he said.

"Why don't you? What if he tries to attack me?" she asked, concerned.

"Then I'll shoot his sorry butt, just go get him."

George heard the door open and a beam of light took over the stairs. Shortly after, a woman came into view.

"Hey, come upstairs. We need to talk."

George stood up and went upstairs following the woman. Upon reaching the top he saw the man sitting at the table, staring at him, gesturing for him to sit down.

"So, you want to get home?" he asked.

"Y...Yes, please," George replied, sitting down at the table across from the man.

"I'll make you a deal. I'll let you talk to who you need to, and you can get them to come get you. But in the meantime, you need to help me around here," the man offered.

George knew he couldn't guarantee Kelsey would come get him, but had to take the chance. If he didn't he would either be stuck here forever or end up six feet under.

"Alright. Give me the radio, but I need to go outside for it to work," George told him.

The woman began to dig in his backpack and handed him the radio and antenna.

George took the radio and antenna and went outside through the backdoor. He set the antenna up and sat down. Turning on the radio, he began to speak, "Kelsey, hello?"

George, what's going on? I've been waiting to hear from you all day. Where are you?

"Well, about that. I need you to come get me," George said, gritting his teeth hoping she would come.

George, what happened that you need me to come get you? You and I both know that you are not at the halfway point. Nowhere near it, at the very least.

"I was trying to get a car, and I got held up. The only way I'm ever going to be leaving here is if you come get me, or I die, and that sure as hell ain't happening."

Kelsey sighed. *I'll be up there in four days. Just let me know where you are in the morning.*

"Thank you, I appreciate it. It probably won't be me telling you where I am, but, I'll make sure you get the information you need," George said.

He began to fold the antenna up but then decided to leave it up. He went back inside and sat back down. "Okay, my friend Kelsey is coming to get me. In the morning, you just need to tell her where this is."

The man grunted. "Alright, back downstairs. I'm going to get some things done."

George went back to the basement and sat against the wall. He fell asleep fairly quickly. Having little sleep the prior night was not good for him.

Chapter 25

Kelsey Davidson

The garage smelled of motor oil and the lingering scent of canned peaches. A welcome smell but one of the few luxuries they'd managed to scavenge last week. Kelsey hefted another bag of supplies into the truck bed, her muscles protesting after days of preparation. Each can made a dull thunk against the metal, a sound that seemed to echo her growing anxiety.

"Preston, Chris, you guys don't have to do this." Already getting warm out, she wiped sweat from her forehead with the back of her hand, leaving behind a smudge of dust. "I can handle this on my own."

The words came out sharper than she'd intended, but the truth was simpler... and more terrifying. She was used to protecting people, not the other way around. The very idea of someone risking their lives for her decision sat in her stomach like a stone.

Chris shifted his weight from foot to foot, the nervous energy radiating off him in waves. His hands opened and closed at his sides, and she could see the internal battle playing out across his face.

Before she could say anything, Chris spoke. "Please, at least let me go. I don't want you to go alone. You heard that guy; he sounds dangerous," Chris said, trying his best to convince her.

That guy. The radio transmission still played in her mind like a broken record. Kelsey studied Chris's face, noting the stubborn set of his jaw that reminded her painfully of Parker.

When had the kid become so determined to throw himself into harm's way? The question must have shown in her expression because Chris straightened his shoulders, trying to look older than his years.

"Fine, I guess, just get what you need, quick. I'll load up food while I wait," Kelsey told him.

Relief flooded Chris's expression followed by a flash of momentary panic as the reality of what he'd volunteered for hit him.

Sure it was the right thing, he said, "Thanks, I'll be right back."

He jogged off toward the house, and Kelsey watched him go before turning back to the truck. She methodically checked each bag: canned goods, medical supplies, ammo, all the essentials of this new world.

Preston's approach was much more silent, but his boots made light scuffing sounds against the garage floor. She bristled when he startled her.

"I understand you would be fine on your own, and I trust that, but I'd rather be safe than sorry. Things are going to be different than two weeks ago when you made the journey here. People are more desperate, and most likely have learned and felt what it's like to kill," Preston explained.

Kelsey's hands stilled on the rope she'd been adjusting with the memory of that trip: the empty highways and abandoned cars; the eerie silence where there should have been life.

"People are more dangerous now," he said, his voice low.

"I guess you're right." The admission came out on a sigh,

her shoulders sagging slightly. "I hadn't thought about that."

The garage door creaked as it opened further, and Parker stepped into view.

"Mom, when will you be back?" Parker asked. The simple question carried so much weight.

Kelsey turned from the truck, looking toward her son. He stood with his arms crossed, trying to appear casual, but she could see the tension in his posture, the way he kept glancing between her and the loaded truck as if memorizing the scene.

"Hopefully, a week. Depends if everything goes smooth. Week and a half at the latest."

The timing felt arbitrary. In this new world time was something they could never really count on. Measured now, not in hours or days, but heartbeats. Moments of safety between the dangers lurking behind the next moment.

"Okay. Remember to be safe and keep an eye out for trouble."

"I know. I will. You need to keep everyone here safe. You and Preston, both," Kelsey said, looking at Preston. "No more stabbings."

He nodded, his hand moving unconsciously to his bandaged arm before looking behind him to see Chris walking over. "Ready to go?"

"I guess," Chris said, stuffing his hastily packed duffle into the truck. "Let's go get this guy."

Kelsey turned to Parker, wrapping him in a hug. "Alright. Be safe, keep Sydney safe."

"I will, same to you, don't get into trouble," his voice was muffled against her shoulder, and she felt him squeeze a little tighter before letting go.

She nodded before climbing into the driver's seat of the truck. Settling into the seat, she took a deep breath, wrapping her hands around the steering wheel and gazing at Parker one last time before they left.

"Everything's going to be alright. Promise. I won't let anything happen to you," Chris's voice came from beside her as he clicked his seatbelt into place. The sound was startlingly normal, a remnant from the time when seatbelts were about traffic accidents, not gunfire and worse.

Kelsey nodded, though her eyes remained fixed on the rearview mirror where she could see Parker and Preston standing in the garage doorway. "I know. It's just, I hate leaving Parker alone again."

The words came out rougher than she'd intended. The truth was, every mile she put between herself and her son felt like tearing away a piece of her heart. The first time she'd left him, ignorance had been a kind of blessing. Now she knew exactly how many things could go wrong.

"He'll be fine. He did fine the first time, and now he has Preston, Leo, his wife, and her mom." Chris's attempt at reassurance was gentle, and she could hear him trying to convince himself as much as her.

"You're right. I should stop thinking about it. Let's just go get George."

The stark familiarity of their neighborhood landscape rolled past the windows. Houses that had once bustled with life now stood empty, their dark windows like hollow eyes. A few showed signs of recent occupation—boarded windows, makeshift fortifications—but most had been abandoned to whatever came next.

"How do you know George again?" Chris asked.

Kelsey kept her eyes forward, focused on the cracked asphalt ahead, moving forward, navigating an abandoned sedan that had been there for weeks. "He's my boss. We weren't too close, but.. I don't want to just leave him on his own."

The understatement felt huge in the confined space of the

truck cab. George was the kind of man who'd called maintenance when his office plant died, who'd never changed a tire in his life, who brought store-bought cookies to office parties and apologized that they weren't homemade. The idea of him alone in this new world was almost unbearable.

"He doesn't know much of this survival stuff. He has a ton of military connections, so he could be helpful to us."

Chris was quiet for a moment, watching the empty landscape roll by. When he spoke, his voice was soft with understanding, "As much as I say we shouldn't bring more people to our group, it is hard just to watch people suffer alone."

"You and me, both." Kelsey's hands tightened on the steering wheel as they passed a burned out house, its blackened shell a reminder of how quickly their old world crumbled.

Behind them in the rearview mirror, the garage grew smaller and smaller until it finally disappeared, taking with it the last glimpse of Parker's worried face, and the fragile safety they'd built together.

Thank you for reading
Please consider leaving a review.

About the Author

Aidan McCollum is a young author who has grown up in Southern Colorado. He found his passion for writing in late 2022 and later began writing in the post-apocalyptic genre, where he has published his debut novel 'Colorado Fall.'

When he isn't writing, he spends his time doing archery with his family, camping, or hunting.